A PITCHER TO
REMEMBER

DON INMAN

Copyright © 2022 Don Inman.

All rights reserved. No part of this book may be reproduced, stored, or transmitted by any means—whether auditory, graphic, mechanical, or electronic—without written permission of both publisher and author, except in the case of brief excerpts used in critical articles and reviews. Unauthorized reproduction of any part of this work is illegal and is punishable by law.

ISBN: 979-8-88640-394-7 (sc)
ISBN: 979-8-88640-395-4 (hc)
ISBN: 979-8-88640-012-0 (e)

Because of the dynamic nature of the Internet, any web addresses or links contained in this book may have changed since publication and may no longer be valid. The views expressed in this work are solely those of the author and do not necessarily reflect the views of the publisher, and the publisher hereby disclaims any responsibility for them.

One Galleria Blvd., Suite 1900, Metairie, LA 70001
1-888-421-2397

Dedication

I would like to thank all those who stood behind me in the process of writing this book. Special thanks also goes to my baby sister, Belinda Inman, who passed away before the completion of this book.

I miss you, girl.

DON INMAN

It all started October 10, 1964, a Saturday morning at about 4:00 A.M. Bryan and Mary Jones became the proud parents of a beautiful brown-skinned baby girl. They named her Adreena. When Adreena started crying at night, the Joneses had to take turns sitting up with her and giving her warm bottles of milk.

Mr. Jones worked at the Montiville Post Office, and Mrs. Jones worked at the Montiville Bank. Now, during the day Adreena would be okay; she would laugh, giggle, and play a lot. However, when nighttime came and it was time for her to go to bed, she would just cry her little eyes out until she got a warm bottle of milk.

Ten months later, Adreena started walking. She was able to play with other kids about her own age. Mr. and Mrs. Jones were sitting on the screened porch one day, and they noticed that Adreena was playing with a softball. She had gotten the softball from Marcus, who lived next door. Marcus's mother, Martha, came outside looking for him. She saw Marcus playing with Adreena, and she thought it was nice. Martha told Bryan that his daughter was a cutie and that she had the cutest smile. Martha said, "She has Mary's eyes, but your smile."

Bryan told Martha thank you. Adreena and Marcus played for a while, and then it was time for Marcus to go inside. Before Martha and Marcus went inside, Martha turned around and asked Adreena for the ball. Adreena looked up at Martha and threw the ball at her face. Bryan looked over at Mary and then said to Martha, "I'm sorry about that." Then he said, "Adreena, you almost hit her right in the face." Adreena just looked up at them and gave a big smile.

Two months passed; Adreena was now three years old. Adreena's mom and dad were putting a surprise birthday party together for her. Mr. Jones called over to the neighbor's house and told Martha and Marcus to bring Adreena back over to the house because they were finished decorating it. When Adreena came in, she had the biggest smile on her face; she couldn't wait to get to the presents. Mr. and Mrs. Jones told everyone that they were going to count to three, and then everyone would sing "Happy Birthday."

After everyone finished singing "Happy Birthday" to Adreena, she began to open her presents. Adreena really enjoyed doing that; she was so excited. Adreena looked inside a big box, and inside there were two little dolls and a big pillow with her name on it to put on her bed when she slept. Adreena continued to look in the box; there were some puzzles and cards with pictures on them still left inside. The cards were for her to use so she could get a head start on trying to figure out how to match pictures together. Mr. and Mrs. Jones thought it would be a good idea for Adreena to start learning at an early age.

After Adreena finished emptying out the box, she started to play with her cards. She picked up one card that had a drawing of a ball on it and started pointing at the picture. Mr. and Mrs. Jones came over and looked at the picture that was in her hand. Mr. Jones said to his wife, "Look, honey, she's going to play softball like you." And Mrs. Jones then said to her husband, "Maybe You never know."

A few more years passed. Adreena was now four years old. Mrs. Jones thought it would be a good idea to enroll Adreena in Mrs. Jackson's Daycare. The one thing Mrs. Jones liked about Mrs. Jackson's Daycare was that it was a learning daycare. Adreena was placed in Mrs. Williams's class. And Mrs. Williams was very excited about Adreena being in her class. Adreena and Mrs. Williams got along very well. Mrs. Williams told Mrs. Jones that Adreena reminded her of her little girl named Miya. When Adreena walked into the classroom, some of the other kids greeted her. And, right then and there, Mrs. Jones knew that

Adreena was in the right class. Mrs. Jones said good-bye to Adreena and left.

The kids took their seats, and Mrs. Williams passed out books to the class. Then Mrs. Williams walked up to the front of the classroom and asked everyone to open their books to page one. Then she went over the name of the town and state they lived in. All the other kids could say the name Montiville, which was located in South Carolina. But when it came time for Adreena to say the name, she had a hard time pronouncing it. Some of the kids laughed and made fun of her. However, that didn't stop Adreena; she was determined to pronounce Montiville the right way. Mrs. Williams told Adreena she had done a good job.

Then Mrs. Williams thought it was time to switch things up a little and maybe take the kids outside. But before she did that, she wanted to see who could spell a few of the words she had on the blackboard without any problems. So Mrs. Williams called on Stephanie, Tony, Bobby, and Sheila. They all could spell the words *pig*, *house*, *boat*, and *walk* without any problems. When it was Adreena's turn to spell the words she stumbled over them, but she managed to do it. Mrs. Williams told everyone, "Good job," and then she took the kids outside.

Some of the kids in the class went to play on the monkey bars, and some went to play on the swings. There was a softball field across the street from the school, and Adreena spotted a girls' softball team practicing on the field. All of the other kids seemed to be having fun playing on the playground. But Adreena was standing at the fence of the school, watching the softball team practice.

Mrs. Williams walked over to the fence where Adreena was standing. She asked Adreena, "What is it?" And with a big smile, Adreena turned and looked at Mrs. Williams and pointed over to the softball field. She told Mrs. Williams that someday she would like to play softball. And Mrs. Williams told her, "That's great, Adreena." Then she gathered up Adreena and the rest of the kids, and they went back inside. Mrs.

Williams then told everyone to put their books away because they were getting ready to go to the library to do some reading.

All of the kids put their stuff away, but Adreena was taking her time and singing to herself. Mrs. Williams asked Adreena, "What are you singing about?" Adreena said it was a song her mother used to sing walking around the house and that it would just keep a smile on her face.

When the kids arrived at the library, Mrs. Williams suggested they find chairs and put them in a circle and sit down because it was story time. After they did that, Mrs. Williams told them each to go pick out a book he or she wanted her to read during story time. The kids picked out books they liked. Adreena came back with a book about a black women softball player name Viola Smith. Adreena showed the book to Mrs. Williams. And then Mrs. Williams told everyone to have a seat because she was going to read the book Adreena had picked out.

Mrs. Williams asked everyone to be quiet, and then she began to read. She said, "This story is about a black woman softball player, and her name is Viola Smith. Viola was born on December 10, 1924, in the town of Stew, Georgia. Viola started playing softball at the age of three, and, boy, she could throw the ball fast! Especially for a four-year-old!

"Every time she went to throw the ball to the batter, they would swing and miss. The catcher would catch it and take her hand out of the glove and shake it. Then the catcher would look at Viola and ask her, 'Where did you learn to throw like that?' Viola told her, 'I have a brother who pitches for the Georgia Hawks Baseball Team. And one of the things I've learned from him is how to pitch.'

"Viola had a spunky way about herself, and that's one of the things the team really liked about her. She also stood up for herself and didn't take anything off of anyone no matter how big they were." While Mrs. Williams was reading the story you could tell Adreena was very interested because she wouldn't stop smiling. Mrs. Williams continued to read. "Viola turned five years old, and she wanted to show her brother that she could pitch like him."

Then all of a sudden, Mrs. Williams said that she was going to stop reading right there for the day and told the class that she would continue to read the story tomorrow. The class lined up; and as they were leaving the library, Adreena went back to the table where Mrs. Williams had left the book. Adreena picked the book up and said to the librarian that she wanted to be just like Viola. Outside, Mrs. Williams looked back to see if everyone was in line. When she saw that Adreena was not there, she called her name, and Adreena came running out of the library.

Mrs. Williams asked her, "Where have you been?" Adreena said that she was just looking at some more books. They finally made it back to the classroom. Mrs. Williams told everyone to start getting their things together because it was time to go home. When Mrs. Jones came to pick Adreena up, she asked Mrs. Williams, "What kind of day did Adreena have?" And Mrs. Williams told Mrs. Jones, "Adreena had a very interesting day. We read a story about a softball player name Viola Smith." Mrs. Jones said, "That's good because it seems like she is really getting into softball. I hope that one day she will make that dream come true."

A few years passed. It was now 1974. Adreena was ten and in the fourth grade. It was coming to the end of the school year; summer was fast approaching; Mr. and Mrs. Jones wondered what they were going to do to keep Adreena busy that summer. One day Mr. Jones was in the den watching TV and trying to read the newspaper at the same time. Mrs. Jones came in and told Mr. Jones that she was getting ready to go to the grocery store to pick up a few things. She asked Adreena if she wanted to come along. Adreena said, "Yes, Mommy."

While on the way to the supermarket, Adreena noticed a sign on the side of the road that announced softball tryouts for girls from nine to twelve years old. When Adreena and her mother arrived at the supermarket, Adreena began to tell her mother about the sign she had seen. Mrs. Jones thought the team would be a good idea; it would give Adreena something to do for the summer.

Back at home, Mrs. Jones asked Adreena, "Do you remember the phone number?" Adreena said yes. Mrs. Jones went into the den where Mr. Jones was. She told him that Adreena had seen a sign along the road announcing softball tryouts and that she thought this was something Adreena could do for the summer. At least it would keep her busy. Mr. Jones asked Mrs. Jones, "Did Adreena get the phone number?" Mrs. Jones said yes. So he said, "Well, let's try it." Mr. Jones dialed the number; the phone rang a couple of times before someone picked it up.

"Hello. This is Coach Rice," said the voice at the other end of the line.

"Hello. My name is Bryan Jones, and I'm calling about the softball tryouts you have for girls ages nine through twelve." Coach Rice said, "Yes, that's right, Mr. Jones. We'll start on Thursday at five o'clock at Jenkins Field." Coach Rice then said to Mr. Jones, "May I ask you a question? Has your daughter ever played softball before?" Mr. Jones answered, "No, she hasn't, but she's a quick learner." Coach Rice said, "That's okay, Mr. Jones. We will work with her; she'll be okay. Just have her at the field by five o'clock on Thursday." Mr. Jones answered, "I'll make sure that she is, Coach Rice. Good-bye."

Mr. Jones told Adreena that everything was set: she would be going to softball tryouts on Thursday at five and would be playing softball over the summer vacation. Adreena jumped up and down for joy; she was excited about playing a game she knew she would enjoy. All she could think about was her favorite softball player, Viola Smith. She couldn't wait until the first day of practice. Mr. Jones nudged Mrs. Jones and then looked at Adreena with a big smile on his face and said, "Don't you think today would be a good time for us to go shopping for all the softball equipment you're going to need to play?" Adreena jumped up and down and shouted, "Yes!"

Mr. and Mrs. Jones and Adreena drove to the mall and went into the Walk Ford Sporting Goods Store. A clerk walked up to them and said, "My name is Sherry. Can I help you with anything?" Mrs. Jones said, "Yes, you can. We're looking for softball equipment." With a smile, Sherry asked, "And who might this be for?" Adreena stepped up with a big grin on her face and said, "It's for me." Sherry said, "Okay. I know exactly what you need. You will need a helmet, baseball shoes, an equipment bag, a couple of bats—and let's not forget a softball glove." Adreena was smiling from ear to ear. She was so happy about becoming a softball player.

Thursday finally came around. Mr. and Mrs. Jones were excited about taking Adreena to softball practice, and Adreena was very excited herself. Mrs. Jones asked Adreena, "Did you finish your homework?" Adreena said, "Yes, Mom. My homework is finished."

Everyone loaded up in the car. All Adreena could think about was the story Mrs. Williams had read about a softball player named Viola Smith.

Finally they arrived at Jenkins Field. Other girls were there with their parents. Everyone looked excited about being there. Coach Rice went over to introduce himself to Adreena and her parents. "Hi, I'm Coach Rice," he said.

"I'm Bryan Jones, and this is my wife Mary," said Adreena's dad. Then Coach Rice asked, "Is this Adreena?" Adreena said hello to Coach Rice. Then he asked her if she had ever played any softball before. Adreena told Coach Rice, "No, but I'm ready to try." Coach Rice said, "That's what I like to hear."

Coach Rice said to all of the parents, "If there is anything you would like to know about me, or if you have any questions about the team, please ask me, and I will try to answer any questions you may have."

So Ms. Fielder, one of the parents, asked Coach Rice, "How many games are they going to be playing?" Coach Rice told Ms. Fielder and the rest of the parents that the girls would play about ten games and one tournament. All of the games would be played locally. "The only game we will play out of town is the tournament game—but we will have to win at least half of the games to qualify for the tournament." Ms. Fielder and the rest of the parents seemed to be happy with Coach Rice.

While the parents were talking with Coach Rice, the girls started talking with each other. Adreena was starting to get to know the other players. One of her teammates came up to her and said, "My name is Josie. I've played softball before; I played first base." Another player came up and said, "Hi, I'm Sally, and I've played third base before." Two other girls walked up to Adreena; their names were Shree and Carmen. They told Adreena that they had never played softball before but they were willing to learn. Adreena told all of the girls her name and that she had never played softball before but she was also ready to learn.

During this whole time, Adreena was thinking to herself that she was not going to be intimidated by any of the other girls that had played before. All she could think of was the story about Viola and how she didn't let anything stop her from doing anything she wanted to do. Coach Rice had finished talking with the parents, and he told the girls to line up because he was going to throw the ball to each of them to see what they could do.

All of the other girls were catching the ball okay; but when Adreena tried, she had a hard time with it, and some of the other girls on the team laughed at her. Adreena wanted to give up, but Coach Rice told her not to worry. "We will have plenty of time to practice," he said. Before practice was over Coach Rice asked the girls to introduce themselves to everyone else on the team. Adreena started first. "My name is Adreena. I'm ten years old."

"Hi I'm Shree."

"I'm Carmen."

The other girls were Josie and Sally, whom Adreena had already met, and Tricia, Brenda, Jackie, Georgia, Jazmine, Candy, Keisha, Paula, and Nicky.

Coach Rice said, "Now that everyone knows each other's names, let's get back to practice. We're only going to be here about ten more minutes." One of the parents asked Coach Rice, "Do you have anyone else helping you?" He said, "Yes, and she's pulling up right now." He introduced his assistant. "Everyone, this is my wife, Rhonda Rice."

Josie said to the team with excitement, "Do you know who that is?" Everyone looked at Josie and said, "No, who is she?"

Josie said she had been on the cover of *Sports Illustrated* for three years in a row; she had been the best women's softball player around. She could've played with any Major League Baseball team. Nicky asked Josie, "What happened?" Josie answered, "She injured her knees sliding into third base in a championship game. She was a pitcher, and she played shortstop."

After Coach Rice finished introducing his wife to everyone, they decided to split the girls up. But before they did that, he told everyone to call him Coach Jeff and call his wife Coach Rhonda to make it easier for everyone.

Half of the girls went with Coach Rhonda, and the others went with Coach Jeff. Coach Rhonda started working with some of the girls to see how well they could catch and throw to each other. On the other side of the field, Coach Jeff had asked three of the girls—Paula, Nicky, and Adreena—to come with him. He told them to line up at the pitcher's mound. He told Nicky to start first, so she got up on the pitcher's mound and threw the ball to Coach Jeff. He said, "Good job!" and told her to try it again. So she threw it to Coach Jeff again, and he said, "That was a great throw—but this time, throw the ball faster."

So Nicky threw the ball again, and this time she threw it very fast. Coach Jeff really liked that. Now it was Paula's turn. She stepped up on the mound, and the first time she threw the ball it almost hit Coach Jeff in the face. Paula put her hand over her mouth and said over and over, "I'm sorry, I'm sorry." Coach Jeff told her that it is okay. "Just straighten it out next time. Now throw it again, but keep your arm straight." Paula tried it again, and this time it hit Coach Jeff's glove right in the center. Coach Jeff seemed to be satisfied with that.

Coach Jeff told Adreena to get up on the pitcher's mound next and throw the ball. Adreena took her time. She looked around and saw that both of her parents were looking at her. Then they turned and looked at each other, and Mrs. Jones said, "Adreena seems to be hesitating for some reason." Coach then asked Adreena again to throw the ball. She said, "Okay, here it comes." Adreena threw the ball, and it hit the coach's glove so hard he pulled his hand out of the glove and shook it.

Adreena's parents looked at each other and started smiling. Coach Jeff looked at Adreena with a surprised look on his face and yelled out to her, "Good throw!" Coach Jeff asked her to do it again. She looked at her glove and started thinking about Viola Smith. Then Adreena threw the ball to Coach Jeff. He caught the ball, and again he had to take his hand out of the glove and shake it. When he looked at his hand he saw that it was red and stinging. Coach Jeff told Adreena, "That's enough for right now." Coach sent the girls over to Coach Rhonda and the rest of the team.

Coach Jeff went over to Adreena's parents to ask them a question: "Are you sure she hasn't played softball or pitched anywhere before?" At the same time Mr. and Mrs. Jones said, "Yes, we're sure. This is Adreena's first time." Coach Jeff told Adreena's parents that they had a special charm on their hands. Coach Jeff signaled to Coach Rhonda to bring all the girls over, and he told them they'd had a great practice. "We have a lot of work ahead of us, but we will get there with more practice. And we will be having practice again on Friday after school. So I'll see you all tomorrow."

Coach Jeff told Adreena and the other girls he had worked with on pitching to try working on their pitching at home with their parents in their spare time. "And also remember to keep your grades up and to continue to do your homework," he added. Coach Rhonda told the girls to keep up the good work. As everyone was leaving, Coach Jeff walked over to Mr. and Mrs. Jones and said to them, "You really have a special girl there, with a lot of talent." Mr. and Mrs. Jones said, "We agree with you. We think she is special too."

As they were leaving the practice field, Adreena climbed into the back of the car, and she noticed a box wrapped in blue wrapping paper. She asked her mom, "What is this?" Mrs. Jones told her to go ahead and open it. Adreena opened the present. It was the book about the black softball player named Viola Smith. Adreena said, "Wow, Mom!" We started reading this book way back when I was in Mrs. Williams's class. Mrs. Jones looks at Adreena and smiled. Adreena told her mom that they had never finished reading it. "But," she said "I'm going to finish it this time."

When the Joneses reached home after stopping to eat dinner, it was getting somewhat late. So Mrs. Jones knew that she had to get Adreena into bed, but Mrs. Jones decided she would read Adreena some of the story about Viola Smith before she went to sleep. She asked Adreena, "Do you remember where Mrs. Williams stopped reading?" Adreena told her mom, "The only thing I can remember in the story is that Viola had a brother who played for a professional baseball team. He was a pitcher for an all-black professional baseball team called the Georgia Hawks, and he was very good."

Mrs. Jones found that part of the story and started reading the book to Adreena:

When Viola finished softball practices and games she would come home and start working on her homework. She knew if she didn't finish her homework, she couldn't play in any softball games. And playing softball was something Viola was very serious about. During the holidays Viola couldn't wait until her brother Demi would came home for the holidays so she could tell him about some of the games she had played in.

Sometimes they would stay up into the late-night hours and talk and not go to bed. Viola was really proud of her brother. She asked him if he would come to one of her games that weekend. He told her, "Yes, sis, I would love to." Viola gave him a big smile and told Demi he was the best brother in the whole wide world.

Demi and Viola finally went to sleep. A few hours later Viola's parents got up. They looked in on their son Demi and saw that he was sound asleep. They went to check on Viola, and they noticed that she wasn't in her bed. Mrs. Smith asked Mr. Smith, "Do you have any idea where she may be?" He told her no. They went back to their son's room and woke him up. Mrs. Smith asked Demi, "Do you know where your sister is?" And with a worried voice Demi said, "No, Mom." Then he asked, "Where do you think she could be?"

Then all of a sudden, they heard a noise outside. They all looked at each other and wondered, *What could that noise be?* It sounded like someone was beating on a rug outside. But it was Viola outside, pitching a softball through an old rubber car tire with an old wooden board at the back of it. Mrs. Smith asked Viola, "What do you think you're doing, young lady?" Viola said "I'm getting ready for my game this Saturday against the Dillon County Bears. They have the best record in the league. And it's our turn to play them."

Viola's mom said, "Viola it is too early in the morning. You need to be getting some rest before you have to get up and get ready for school." Viola told her mom, "I know! I know!" Her father said, "You heard your mom!"

Mrs. Jones thought this would be a good place in the book to stop reading, so she told Adreena, "That's enough of the story about Viola for tonight. We can read more later on; but right now, you need to get to sleep. She gave Adreena a kiss on the side of the face. Adreena gave her mother a big hug.

Mrs. Jones was getting ready to leave when Adreena asked her to please send her daddy in. I want to give him a big hug. After Mr. and Mrs. Jones left, Adreena went to sleep. Both parents left her room, smiling at one another, and said, "We have a special little someone on our hands, don't we?"

The next morning, Friday, Adreena was already up and eating cereal for breakfast when her parents got up. Mr. and Mrs. Jones asked

A PITCHER TO REMEMBER

Adreena, "Why are you up so early?" She said, "I'm just excited about going to practice today after school." Mrs. Jones said to her, "Remember, your grades come first." Adreena said, "Yes, Mommy, I know." Then Adreena told her mom, "Someday, I'm going to be like Viola." Her mother said, "That's great, dear." Mrs. Jones and Adreena grabbed their things and headed out the door.

They arrived at Adreena's school, and Adreena got out of the car. Then she turned around and told her mother good-bye. Mrs. Jones looked back at Adreena and said, "Good-bye, dear." And then with a big smile on her face, she said to herself, "Lord, what do I have on my hands?"

As Adreena was making her way into the school, she ran into one of her teammates, Nicky. "Are you ready to go to practice," Adreena asked. Nicky said yes. Then the two of them started walking to their class together. They both had Spanish. Their teacher's name was Mrs. Rachel Carlos. She was from Mexico, but she came to the United States because she wanted to teach kids in the States.

Mrs. Carlos asked the kids to take out their Spanish books and turn to page twelve. She wanted them to learn some new words in Spanish. Mrs. Carlos thought it would be very nice if the kids could learn some of her language and have fun with it. She knew it was part of the daily class work, but these words had very special meaning to them.

At lunchtime, Adreena and Nicky walked to the cafeteria together and ran into some more of their teammates. Paula, Josie, and Jazmine were all laughing about a joke Paula had told them. Adreena asked, "What are you guys laughing about?" Paula said, "It was a joke I told." Nicky said, "What was the joke about?" Paula said, "Which president wore the tallest hat?" Adreena said, "I don't know." Paula said, "It was the one with the tallest head." The girls started laughing so hard they forgot about where they were.

The girls finally made it to lunch, and they saw some more of their teammates: Candy, Keisha, and Georgia. They asked Adreena and the others, "What's up?" Paula said, "Nothing, just school." The girls got in line to get their lunches. After they had gotten their lunches, they saw Sally, Carmen, Tracie, Brenda, and Jackie sitting at a table. So they sat down, and the whole team was together. Everyone started eating, talking, and laughing; they all knew that there was only so much time left to eat.

Adreena started eating, and then she pulled out her favorite book to read while she was eating. It seemed like the other girls were into the jokes Paula was telling. Adreena started reading where her mother had left off in the book:

It was time for Viola to get up and get ready for school. Mrs. Smith dropped her off, and as Viola walked up to the school, she noticed that some of her friends from her softball team were playing on the playground. And it looked like they had a game of softball going. Susie Mulligan saw Viola walking up and yelled, "Hey, Viola! You want to play?" Viola yelled back, "Yeah!" She put her books down and noticed that the clock on the school wall showed that they only had thirty minutes before school would start.

Viola walked up to her teammate Susie, and Susie asked her, "Do you want to pitch?" Viola said, "Sure, no problem." Then Viola told Wilma, another teammate, "If you are going to be catching my pitches, you had better make sure you have some extra padding in that glove, because you are going to need it." Wilma said, "Just throw, I'm ready." And then Viola told Lucy, another one of her teammates, who was getting ready to bat, "Make sure you say your prayers." Lucy looked at Viola with a puzzled look. Then Viola wound up and pitched. Lucy swung and missed. Viola threw the ball again. Lucy swung and missed again. One of the teachers from the school just happened to be watching from a window. It was Mr. Lonnie Rutherford; he was the favorite math teacher at Burnsfield Middle School.

Viola threw her third pitch; Lucy swung and missed that one too. Then Lucy and the rest of Viola's teammates started laughing and gave

Viola a pat on the back. There was one more girl who wanted to hit; she wasn't a teammate. She said to Viola, "Where do you think you're going?" It was Margret Filmner, the tallest girl in the school. You see, Margret played on one of the local teams, and she had hit the winning home run that helped them win the state tournament.

Lucy walked up to Viola and said, "Are you sure you want to do this?" Viola asked Lucy, "How much time do we have before the schoolbell rings, and we have to go in?" Lucy said, "Five minutes." Viola smiled at Lucy and said, "It will only take me three minutes to strike her out." Viola dug deep in the dirt; she wound up and then threw the ball.

Margret hit the ball, but it went foul. Then Margret yelled at Viola and said, "Girl, you don't stand a chance!" Viola looked at Margret and smiled. Then she threw her second ball. Margret hit it—but, yet again, it went foul. Viola cleaned the mound off, and again dug in—even deeper this time. Wilma gave her a signal to throw a curveball. Viola nodded her head okay and smiled; she knew it was time to take care of business.

Viola threw the curve ball. Margret saw the ball coming and opened her eyes wide. She swung and missed this time. When that ball got past Margret you could feel the wind behind it. Everyone who was on the playground jumped up and started cheering for Viola. And Mr. Rutherford couldn't believe what had just happened. Margret walked up to Viola and told her, "You got lucky this time." The school bell rang. It was time for Viola and her friends and the other students to go inside.

Adreena had to stop reading her book. Lunchtime was over. Adreena and the rest of the girls had to get to their next class. Paula was still telling jokes on her way to class.

Adreena walked into her next class: math, with Mr. Barber. Adreena started to sit down; but when she took her book bag off her shoulder, her favorite book fell out and onto the floor. Mr. Barber bent down and picked the book up. Then he asked Adreena, "What is this?" She said, "A book my mother gave to me." Mr. Barber said, "I see you like softball." Adreena said, "Yes, I do." Mr. Barber asked her, "What position do you play?" Adreena replied, "I am a pitcher." Mr. Barber told her that he had been a pitcher also when he played baseball in high school, so if she needed any help with her pitching she should just let him know. Mr. Barber then told the class to take out their math notes from the day before He added, "Remember, class, you have a math test coming up next Friday."

Adreena knew that it was important to do well in school; her mother and father were serious about her keeping up her grades. She knew it was either that or no softball. Adreena went on to finish the rest of her classes; and then the last bell of the day rang, and it was time to go home. Carmen asked Adreena, "Are you coming to practice today?" Adreena told her that she wouldn't miss it for the world and that she was excited about going to practice. Both Carmen's and Adreena's parents picked them up from school and took them to practice. They were the first ones there. Then the rest of the girls started to show up. Coach Jeff said that he wanted to talk with all of the girls before practice started.

Coach Jeff wanted to let the girls know that they were going to have their first game in two weeks. So he needed to go ahead and start putting them in the positions they would be playing. Coach Rhonda told the girls, "We have a great team, and I know that we're going to have a great season." The girls looked at each other and started smiling. Then Coach Jeff told the girls that they would have uniforms in a week.

Nicky asked Coach Jeff, "What colors are the uniforms?" Coach told the girls the uniforms would be gray and white with numbers in black. The girls seemed to be really happy about the uniform colors. Coach Jeff split the girls up again for practice. He wanted to make sure that they knew what positions they were going to play. He wanted Adreena, Nicky, Paula, and Tracie to go straight to the pitcher's mound. Coach Rhonda told the rest of the girls to come with her.

Coach Rhonda asked Josie, Jazmine, and Candy to start throwing the ball to each other. And then she told the other girls to get out in the field. "I'm going to start hitting the ball to see how you are at grounding the ball. And then I want you to throw it to the third baseman, which will be Keisha. And I want you to throw it very hard and fast." Coach Rhonda then said to everyone, "Please pay attention out here because, if you don't, you could get hurt really bad—so, be careful." Coach Rhonda hit the ball to Georgia, and she ran back and caught it and threw it to Keisha, who caught it easily. Coach Rhonda said to Keisha, "Good job."

Then Coach Rhonda hit the ball to Sally and yelled out to her, "Keep your feet under you!" Sally caught the ball without any problems. While Coach Rhonda was in another area of the field practicing with her group of girls, Coach Jeff was working with the catchers and pitchers. Coach Jeff asked Nicky to start pitching first. Nicky threw a pitch to Coach Jeff; but she threw the ball far outside the batter's box. Coach Jeff told Nicky, "That's okay. You will get better." Nicky threw another pitch, and it went straight into Tracie's glove. Coach Jeff told her, "Good job—now try one more pitch." Nicky stepped up and then back and threw very fast. Tracie caught the ball and started smiling. "What a great pitch!" she said. Nicky felt really good about herself.

Coach Jeff then called Paula up to pitch. But when Coach Jeff looked at the pitcher's mound, Paula was not there. Coach Jeff turned and looked over to the dugout. Paula was laughing with Adreena and telling jokes. Coach Jeff yelled her name, "Paula! Could you please go to the pitcher's mound?" When Paula heard her name she hurried out of the dugout. She picked up some sand from the mound and rubbed it on the ball. Then she threw the ball straight to Tracie's glove.

Coach Jeff said, "That was a good pitch" Paula's mother, Mrs. Lynn Jackson, yelled out, "That's the way to go, baby!" Paula looked over at her mom and started smiling. Coach Jeff told Paula, "So, I see you can do something else besides tell jokes." And Paula said, "Sure, coach," with a smile on her face. Coach Jeff told Paula, "I want your next pitch to be nice and fast." Then he asked Tracie, "Are you okay?" She said, "Sure, coach. I feel good." Paula stared at Tracie and gave her a mean look. Tracie said, "What is wrong, Paula?" Paula said, "I am trying to figure out how many monkeys it takes to screw in a lightbulb." Coach Jeff said, "What?" Then Tracie and Coach Jeff started laughing, and everyone else did too. Still laughing, Coach Jeff told Paula, "It's time to get back to practice now." So Paula threw the ball, and Tracie caught it and fell back, still laughing at Paula's joke. "I got it," she said, with a smile on her face.

Coach Jeff was trying to keep a straight face as he asked Paula, "Do you ever stop?" Paula looked back at the coach and smiled. Adreena looked at Paula, and she couldn't do anything but smile. Now it was Adreena's turn to pitch. Coach Jeff asked Adreena to take a couple of deep breaths before she started. She did, and then Adreena yelled out very loudly, "Coach, I'm ready!" Coach Jeff told her to go ahead and throw the ball.

Adreena stepped back and looked around; she wanted to make sure that there were no distractions to interrupt her when she got ready to pitch. Adreena then threw the ball straight into Tracie's glove. Tracie said, "What you trying to do, hurt my hand?" Adreena looked over at her mom and dad, smiling with a surprised look on her face, and then shrugged her shoulders. Then Adreena yelled to Tracie, "Are you okay?" And Tracie yelled back, "I'll be okay!"

Coach asked Adreena, "Where did you learn to throw like that?" She said "From my dad." Then Adreena threw her second pitch, and it came harder than the first one. Tracie had to take her glove off again. Mrs. Jones asked Mr. Jones, "Have you been teaching her to pitch like that?" And Mr. Jones said, "Yeah, I've been teaching her, but nothing like that." Adreena's parents just looked at each other, smiled, laughed, and then said, "Where does she get it from?"

Coach Jeff asked Adreena to throw one more pitch. Tracie turned around and looked at Coach Jeff and asked him, "Are you serious?" He said, "Sure I am." Tracie said, "But she is going to burn my hand with that ball." Before Adreena started to throw her last pitch, Tracie's mom,

Mrs. Baxter, asked Coach Jeff if Tracie could use her batting glove to put in her catcher's glove. Coach Jeff said, "That is a great idea." Then Coach Jeff said, "Okay, Adreena, go ahead and throw the ball." This time Adreena didn't hold back. She let the ball go, and again it went straight down the lane right into Tracie's glove. Adreena yelled out to Tracie, "Did it hurt this time?" Tracie said, "Just a little, but I'm okay." Coach Jeff just stood there for a moment and shook his head in amazement at Adreena's pitching ability.

Coach Jeff then thought it was time for all of the players to come together. So he waved to Coach Rhonda and told her to bring the rest of the girls over by the batter's box. He wanted to talk with all of them. Coach Jeff told the team, "I think we have a great team, so we should be able to do very well this season." Then Coach Rhonda said, "Everyone is doing a good job playing their positions." Then Coach Jeff told the girls they would have their first game that Saturday against a team called the Carolina Beavers. Paula asked Coach Jeff, "What is the name of our team?" Coach Rhonda said, "We are the Montville Cubs." All of the girls started yelling and jumping up and down. Coach Jeff told everyone to be at Jenkins Field at three o'clock on Saturday afternoon. He said the game wouldn't start until three thirty, but he would like for everyone to be at the field at three.

All of the parents were excited about seeing the girls play in Saturday's game. Everyone left practice and went home. Adreena was really excited about playing in the game on Saturday. She was so excited she asked her mother if she could stay up a little longer before going to bed. Mrs. Jones said, "Yes, but only for a little while." Adreena started reading her book about Viola Smith, her favorite softball player:

After school was over with, Viola walked home to tell her mom that some of the girls from the softball team were going to walk over to Lucy's house to do some homework. Viola asked her mom if she could go too, and her mom said yes. Viola told her mom that she would call her from Lucy's house to pick her up when they finished their homework. While walking to Lucy's house, the girls noticed an all-black women's baseball team on Murphy's Field. The girls were amazed at the way the team was practicing and how they were throwing the ball to each other. Viola couldn't believe how hard the pitcher was throwing the ball to the catcher. Susie said, "Can you believe the teamwork they have? Boy, they are good!"

While the girls were standing there watching the team practice through the fence, one of the players from the team hit the ball over the fence. Viola noticed that the ball rolled into some bushes. So she walked over to the bushes, picked up the ball, and threw it back over the fence to the outfielder. The coach of the team noticed how Viola threw the ball back over the fence.

The coach walked over to Viola and asked her what her name was, and she told him. And the coach then said to Viola, "You've got a pretty good arm there, kid." And he asked her, "Where did you learn to throw like that?" Viola said, "My brother." The coach asked her, "Who is he, and does he play?" Viola said, "Demi Smith. And, yes, he plays with a team called the Georgia Hawks." The coach said, "Well, let me tell you, he is doing a good job with you." Then the coach asked Viola, "These your friends?" She said yes. Viola introduced them to the coach one by one. This is Hattie, Wilma, Mable, Louise, Margie, Lucy, Mattie, Mary, Amy, Susie, and Thelma. We play on the same softball team.

Viola asked the coach, "What is your name?" And he said, "My name is Coach Roy Davidson." Then Viola asked him, "What is the name of your baseball team?" The coach said, "The Junction Clowns." Then Lucy said with a grimace on her face, "The clowns?" Coach Roy said, "Yep, that's right—the clowns." Coach Roy told the girls that he had been coaching this team for about seven years. Then Coach Roy asked the girls, "Do you want to meet a few of my players?" The girls' eyes got big, and at the same time, they all said, "Yes!"

Coach Roy called three of his players over to the fence where he was standing with the girls and introduced a few of his players to them. "This is Mary Johnson, and they call her Peanut; she pitches for the team. And this is Tonya Stone; she plays second base. And this is Cynthia Morgan; they call her Cindy, and she also plays second base, but we have her working out as a shortstop."

All three of the Junction Clowns players asked Viola and the rest of the girls, "Are you pretty good ball players?" They all answered yes at the same time. Mary of the Junction Clowns asked Viola and her teammates if they would like to practice with them sometime if it was alright with Coach Roy. The girls said yes. Coach Roy told Mary, "Not so fast, now; these girls play softball not baseball." Tonya said, "We know, coach, but at least we can help them out a little." "Well, let me think about it," Coach Roy said. Then he told Viola and her teammates, "We will be here a few more days. We have about six more games to play here. So if you're around, stop by later in the week, and we will give you a few lessons to help you out." And with excitement they all said, "Okay!"

Viola then told Coach Roy, "We have to get going now; we have homework to do. But we won't forget to come by." Viola and her teammates told Coach Roy and the players good-bye.

Viola and the girls were amazed at meeting Coach Roy and some of the players. That was all they could talk about on the way to Lucy's house. They finally made it there, and Mrs. White, Lucy's mother, asked the girls if they wanted anything to eat. Everyone answered yes. She also asked the girls why everyone was in such a good mood. They told her that they had just met a professional baseball team called the Junction Clowns—and boy, they were really good! After the girls finished their homework, Viola called her mother to pick her up.

Then Mrs. Smith and some of the other mothers started showing up at Lucy's house to pick up their kids. Viola got into the car, and Mrs. Smith asked Viola, "What are you so excited about?" She said, "Mom, you will never guess what happened to us today!" And with even more excitement Viola said, "Guess what, Mom! Guess what!"

Mrs. Smith said, "What, Viola? What is it?" Viola said, "Mom, we met a professional baseball team today!"

Smiling, Mrs. Smith asked her, "How did that happen?" Viola explained, "We were walking from school to Lucy's house, and we saw a baseball team practicing at Murphy's Field, and one of the players hit a baseball over the fence. I went to get the ball and threw it back over the fence. And the coach of the Junction Clowns noticed how I threw the ball back over the fence. He told me I have a good throwing arm. He also introduced me and my teammates to some of his players. And, oh, Mom! The best part is he said that we could practice with them. He said he would give us a few pointers on the game. I can't wait! You know, Mom, I wonder if he would give us tickets to some of their games?"

Mrs. Smith said, "You never know, Viola. He might." When Mrs. Smith and Viola arrived at home, Viola swung opened the door of the car and ran inside. She wanted to share the good news with her father and Demi.

Demi told Viola that the Junction Clowns was one of the best teams in the league. Demi also told Viola that their team the Georgia Hawks had practice with the Junction Clowns twice that year. "And they beat us both times!" Viola was so happy about what had happened to her and her teammates.

Adreena saw that it was getting late, so she stopped reading and left the book on her bed. She had a game in the morning.

On Saturday morning Adreena was the first one up. She was so excited about her first softball game. Adreena went to her parent's bedroom; she opened up the door and peeked in. Then she ran and jumped into the middle of the bed and woke her mom and dad up. Her dad asked her, "Are you okay?" Adreena said, "Yes, Daddy, I'm just excited about the game today." Adreena looked at her mom and said, "Come on! Get up! We have to get to the softball field." Both of her parents looked at each other and smiled. They pointed at each other and said, "That's your daughter."

A PITCHER TO REMEMBER

While they were eating breakfast, the telephone started ringing. Mrs. Jones answered it, and it was Paula. She asked, "Is Adreena up yet?" Mrs. Jones said, "Yes, she is, and she's eating breakfast right now." Mrs. Jones turned and looked at Adreena, and she said, "It is the jokester, Paula." Mr. Jones started laughing. Adreena picked up the phone and said, "Hi, Paula" And Paula said, "Hey, Adreena! Are you ready to play today?" With enthusiasm, Adreena said, "Yes, I am!" Adreena asked Paula, "What about you?" Paula said, "Girl, you know it." Mrs. Jones said to Adreena, "Tell Paula you have to finish your breakfast." Before Adreena and Paula finished their conversation, Paula told Adreena, "I have a joke for you." Adreena said, "Oh, boy! What is it?"

Paula said, "Can a chicken cross the road?" Adreena said, "What?!" Paula said again, "Can a chicken cross the road?" Adreena answered no. Paula said, "Sure they can, if they wait their turn." Adreena started laughing. Mrs. Jones said, "I do not know what her mother is going to do with her." Adreena returned to the table after talking with Paula. She couldn't stop smiling about the joke that Paula had just told her. After Adreena finished her breakfast, Mrs. Jones told her to go and get dressed for the game.

As Adreena was getting dressed, there was a knock on her bedroom door. Adreena asked, "Who is it?" "It's me. Daddy." Adreena said, "Come in," and then asked, "What's wrong, Dad? Why do you have that look on your face?" He said, "I can remember the very first day you were born. You were so small … now look at you." Mr. Jones continued, "I'm so proud of you." Adreena gave him a big smile and a big hug. Mrs. Jones came in and said, "Alright, you two. It's time to get out of here." The three of them walked out to the garage and got into the car.

Just as Mr. Jones started to pull away, Adreena yelled, "Dad! Stop! Please stop!" Mr. Jones asked, "What is it, Adreena?" She said, "I left my book." "What book, Adreena?" She said, "My book about Viola!" Adreena got out of the car and ran up the stairs and started looking for the book. "Where is it? Where is it? Where can it be?" she asked herself aloud. She looked under the bed and behind her closet door. Then she put her hands on top of her head, stopped, stood still for a second, and said, "Where could it be?" Then she walked over to her bed, pulled the covers back, and found the book. Adreena then gave a big sigh of relief, ran back downstairs, and got back into the car.

"We can go. Now I am ready to play a good game," Adreena said. On their way to the game Adreena wanted to start reading more of her book about Viola Smith, whom she was starting to admire very much. But there wasn't enough time for her to really get into the book, because the field wasn't far from their house, so she just held onto it. It seemed like Adreena was starting to see some of Viola in herself.

They made it to the softball field. Adreena didn't want to let go of her book. She knew it was time to get ready to play, but she still brought the book with her. Mr. and Mrs. Jones and some of the other parents were amazed at some of the other team's uniform colors and players. They knew they were in for a long day.

Coach Jeff and Coach Rhonda called their team together to discuss a few things with them. Coach Jeff wanted to make sure the girls were okay and not nervous. He told the girls, "You will be okay," and Coach Rhonda said, "Just remember what we taught you in practice." To be sure that everyone on his list was there, Coach Jeff started calling all of the players names out loud, and he asked them to say "here" when they heard their names. He started with Nicky, Josie, Jazmine, Candy, Keisha, Georgia, Adreena, Sally, Carmen, Tracie, Brenda, Jackie, Shree, and Paula. When Coach Jeff didn't hear Paula say here, he said, "Where is Paula?" Everyone looked for her.

Keisha said, "There she is." Everybody turned and looked. Paula was standing in the middle of a circle of girls from the other teams, laughing and telling jokes. Coach Jeff and Coach Rhonda yelled, "Paula! Please get over here!" Coach Jeff told the girls, "We're getting ready to play next." Adreena looked at her parents with a big smile; she knew that she was in for a lot of fun.

Coach Jeff told everyone what position they were going to play. He told Josie to play first base. "Jazmine will play second base. Keisha, you play third base. Candy, you play shortstop. Sally, you're in center field. Carmen, you play left field. Tracie, you're the catcher. Georgia, you're in right field, and Paula, I'm going to start you off pitching."

Then Coach Jeff told the other girls—Brenda, Jackie, Shree, Adreena, and Nicky—to have a seat in the dugout, until he was ready to change out a player for another in the game. Adreena thought that until the coach changed players, she would take her book out and read more about Viola:

Saturday morning came around, and Viola's team, the Burnsfield Cats, had a game to play. They were going to be playing the Dillon County Bears. This was a team that the Burnsfield Cats had feared, but they knew they were going to have to play sooner or later, and it was much sooner than later. All of the girls from the Burnsfield Cats team showed up at the field ready to play. They began getting ready to take their positions out on the field. Their coach, Melvin Percy, had played professional baseball for the Negro League team.

He had retired years ago from the league, but Coach Melvin said he always knew that one day the Negro League would turn professional. And Coach Melvin was the kind of coach that had the philosophy that if you worked hard at something, one day it would pay off. Coach Melvin went over the positions each of his players was going to play.

Coach Melvin put Hattie on first base and Lucy on second base. Mable was shortstop; Louise would be playing third base; Mattie, right field; Mary, center field; Amy, left field; Wilma, catcher; and Susie was the starting pitcher. Viola, Margie, and Thelma would be relief pitchers, but for now they would be in the dugout. Coach Melvin told them to just hang in there—they would get their turns.

The game started, and the first batter up from the Dillon County Bears was Helen Mayfield. Now, Helen was the type of player to get nervous while getting ready to hit. She also talked to herself—for what reasons no one knew—but that was her thing. Susie knew all she had to do was throw the ball straight at Helen, and she would clam up. Susie threw the first pitch, and Helen grabbed the bat really tight, swung, and missed. Susie pitched again. Helen stared at the ball all the way to the bat, and she missed again. Susie wiped the sweat from her forehead.

Then Wilma gave Susie a different signal for a pitch to throw next. Susie smiled and nodded her head in agreement with the pitch. Susie set up and threw the side-curved ball. But this time Helen hit the ball, and it went up and straight out to Mary in center field. Mary missed the ball, and Helen made it to first base. Coach Melvin yelled out to Susie and Mary, "That's alright! We'll get the next one!" The next player up to bat was Johnnie Curtains. Johnnie stayed quiet; she really did not say a whole lot. The only time she opened her mouth was when she didn't like certain people. And with that look on her face you could tell she really didn't like Susie.

Susie looked at Coach Melvin; he gave her a signal to strike Johnnie out. Coach Melvin didn't want to waste any time with Johnnie. He wasn't really sure about her. Susie stepped back and looked around. She threw the first pitch, and Johnnie hit the ball between first and second base. Hattie and Lucy missed the ball. Helen went to second, and Johnnie made it to first base. Coach Melvin was starting to worry; he called time out and walked over to the pitcher's mound to talk with Susie.

Coach Melvin asked Susie if she was okay. And Susie told him that she was nervous because it was her first game, but she was going to be alright. Coach Melvin walked back to the dugout, and he took his hat off and wiped the sweat off his forehead. Then he said to himself, "I can't believe this—it's the first game, and I'm already this nervous."

The next person to bat was Joyce Richards; she would yell every word that came out of her mouth. You would think she had a hearing problem, but that was just her personality. Susie knew it was time to stop playing around. The first two balls Susie threw, Joyce missed. The last pitch Susie threw, Joyce hit it, and it went straight toward third base. Louise caught the ball and then dropped it. Joyce made it to first base; Johnnie advanced to second base, and Lucy advanced to third base

Now the bases were loaded. Coach Melvin didn't know what to think. It was the bottom of the first inning. The bases were loaded, no outs. Coach Melvin called time out again. And then he walked to the pitcher's mound and asked Susie for the ball and told her, "Good job." Everyone clapped for Susie as she left the pitcher's mound. Coach Melvin knew she had done her best, but he knew it was time to make a change.

The next pitcher that he called out was Viola Smith. She walked to the pitcher's mound where Coach Melvin was standing. He told Viola, "You need to strike the next three players out. Do you think you can do that?" Viola asked him, "Do you believe in miracles?" As Coach Melvin was handing Viola the ball he asked her, "What are you trying to say?" Viola just looked at him and smiled. Coach Melvin walked away with a puzzled look on his face.

To warm up, Viola threw a few balls to Wilma. Then she yelled out to the umpire, "I'm ready!" The next two players up to bat were the Henry twins, Pam and Pamela. The one crazy thing about those twins was their hair: they didn't want anything to touch their hair, so they didn't believe in wearing helmets. They were afraid that it would damage their hair! Viola knew it wouldn't take long for her to strike the two sisters out.

Pam was up to bat first. Viola threw her first pitch, and Pam missed. Wilma threw the ball back to Viola. Then Viola threw the ball again, and again Pam missed. Wilma yelled out to Viola, "Same thing!" Viola nodded her head in agreement. Viola threw the third pitch; Pam swung and struck out. Viola said to herself, "Two more outs ... just two more outs."

The next person up at bat is Pam's twin sister, Pamela. Viola didn't want to waste any time with Pamela. Viola threw her first pitch. Pamela swung and missed. Wilma threw the ball to Viola, but as Viola was getting ready to pitch, the umpire called time. The reason was that Pamela had asked her sister for a small mirror to look at her hair; she wanted to make sure that her curls hadn't fallen. The umpire signaled over to the coach of the Dillon County Bears to keep his players inside the dugout.

The umpire told Viola to go ahead and throw the ball. Viola did just that, and Pamela missed again. Then Pamela yelled out to Viola, "You've got one more time to throw that ball at me like that! One more time!" Viola looked over at her coach and then smiled and threw the ball. Pamela swung again and missed—strike three, and she was out. Pam met her twin sister with a mirror, and both of them stopped to look at their hair before going into the dugout. Viola, Wilma, and the umpire all shook their heads. Then Wilma ran out to the pitcher's mound and gave Viola a big hug. Both of them smiled and laughed, feeling really happy about what had just happened.

Then all of a sudden, Mary came running up to them from center field saying, "Hey! Hey! Hey, girls! Hey, girls! Look at whose up next to hit!" Viola and Wilma slowly turned around, and then both of them looked at each other and started shaking their heads. They couldn't believe it; it was Margret Filmner. They did not have any idea Margret played for the Dillon County Bears. Coach Melvin called time out again. He asked Viola, "What's wrong?" She told her coach, "This girl can hit. She's the best in the league." Coach Melvin told Viola, "Just take your time with each pitch, and you can get her out."

Viola said, "Okay, Coach, let's do it." Viola got ready to throw the first pitch; Margret stared at her with great intensity. Viola threw the ball. The umpire yelled, "Strike one!" Everybody on Viola's team was breathing hard, nervous about what was going to happen with the next swing. Viola wound up again and let the ball go. Margret swung and missed again. "Strike two!"

Everyone on the team wiped the sweat from their foreheads. Wilma yelled to Viola, "Take care of business!" Viola threw the third pitch.

A PITCHER TO REMEMBER

This time Margret hit the ball out toward third base. Coach Melvin and everyone else on the team yelled, "Go foul! Go foul!" The ball crossed the yellow line over by third base, and the umpire yelled, "Foul ball!"

Viola knew this could be her last chance to strike Margret out, so she started thinking about some of the pitches her brother Demi had showed her at home. Then Viola remembered a pitch Demi had showed her called the Toss-Up. She stepped up to the mound, and then she looked over at Hattie on first base. She stepped back from the mound plate like she was going to throw the ball fast, but it went to Margret slowly. Margret had a mean look on her face like she could send the ball straight to space.

Margret swung at it as hard as she could—but she missed. The umpire yelled, "Strike three!" Margret was not very pleased about Viola striking her out. Viola and her team were happy that they had held off the Bears in the top of the second inning. Now it was time for the Burnsfield Cats to hit and show the other team what they could do. Coach Melvin said he wanted to talk with the team before they started hitting.

Adreena had to stop reading and put her book down and get back to her game. The Montiville Cubs were playing a really good game against the Carolina Beavers. The game was tied four to four, and the Montiville Cubs had two outs on the Carolina Beavers. They were at the bottom of the fifth inning, and the bases were loaded. Coach Jeff wanted to change out pitchers. He called Adreena over and asked her, "Are you ready?" Adreena told Coach Jeff that she was feeling okay; she was ready.

The next person to hit from the Beavers team was Sandy Johnson. She was determined to hit the ball really hard. The Beavers coach, Lester Ames, told Sandy to watch the ball. Adreena looked in the stands at her parents, and both of them had big smiles on their faces. They could not believe it; their daughter was pitching in this game. Adreena threw her first pitch to Sandy, who missed, The umpire yelled, "Strike one!" Tracie threw the ball back to Adreena. Second pitch. "Strike two!"

Adreena thought about what she had to do. She wiped the mound plate off and threw the ball really fast. Sandy's knees were shaking like leaves in the wind. She swung at the ball and missed again. "Strike three!" The crowd jumped up, and everyone was yelling. Adreena couldn't believe what she had just done.

The Montville Cubs had won their first game. Mr. and Mrs. Jones came running over to Adreena; they could not believe what their little girl had done. Coach Jeff told everyone they played a good game. He asked Coach Rhonda if she had anything to say. She said, "Girls, all of you played a really good game, and you had great defense out there. Keep up the good work, girls. We're proud of you."

After the game was over with, all of the Montville Cubs players left the field and went home. As Adreena and her parents were on their way home Mr. and Mrs. Jones continued to tell Adreena what a great job she and her teammates had done that day. Mr. Jones told Adreena to keep up the good work. "This could get you a scholarship for college," he added.

They finally reached home. Mrs. Jones told Adreena to go upstairs and get out of her uniform, so she could wash it and get it ready for the next game. She also told Adreena to take a shower before it got too late. Adreena was so excited about that day's game. She ran upstairs and took a shower. Then she came back down and went to the living room with her book in hand. Mrs. Jones was in the laundry room. She picked up Adreena's uniform, looked at it, and shook her head in amazement.

Then Mrs. Jones walked into the living room. Mr. Jones had fallen asleep in his favorite chair with a book in his hands. And Adreena had fallen asleep on the couch with her favorite book (the one about Viola Smith, of course) in her hands.

Mrs. Jones woke Mr. Jones up and asked him to carry Adreena upstairs to her bedroom. He laid her down in her bed, and then Mr. and Mrs. Jones whispered to each other, "We have a champion on our hands."

By age fifteen, Adreena had moved on to Montville High School, home of the Wild Tigers. It was the 1980s now. The very first day of school Adreena walked down the hallway and wondered whether she would see some of the old gang from middle school. One of the coaches from the Montville High School softball team recognized Adreena, so he stopped her and introduced himself.

"Hi, my name is Coach Wayne Lawson, and I coach the girls' softball team here. I've heard a great deal about you. We're having tryouts for the team, and if you're interested I would like for you to try out. The tryouts will be two weeks from today."

Adreena gave the coach a big smile and said, "Okay, I'll be there." After Adreena and Coach Lawson talked, she continued to walk down the hallway. Someone yelled after her, "Adreena! Adreena!" She turned around and saw that it was Paula. They were so happy to see each other. Paula said, "Adreena, can you believe it? We're in high school now, girl."

Paula asked Adreena, "What classes do you have?" Adreena told her, "History, math, English, P.E., and biology." Adreena ask Paula about her classes, and Paula said, "The usual." Adreena said, "Paula, let me see your schedule." After looking it over, she said, "It looks like you and I have at least one class together." And Paula said, "Boy, we're going to have fun this year." Adreena asked Paula, "Are you still telling crazy jokes? Because you know this is high school now, and we're older, and this is new for both of us." Paula just smiled. Then Adreena and Paula said to each other, "See you in science class."

So after they had finished their other classes, Paula and Adreena met up in the hallway and walked together to their last class of the day. Paula said, "Adreena, let's sit here." Both of them sat down. Mrs. S. Mulligan walked in after the bell rang. She said, "Good morning. I'm Mrs. Mulligan, your science teacher, and this is classroom number 541 in the Science Building. Please stay seated where you are for now, but I'm going to be making different seating arrangements. I will call your name to let you know where you will be sitting for the remainder of the year."

While she was doing that, Paula looked like she was making some new friends already. Adreena noticed a picture on the side of the blackboard. It showed a group of girls in softball uniforms; on the uniforms was printed "Burnsfield Cats High School Softball Team."

Adreena tried to get Paula's attention to show her, but Paula was too busy talking to her new friends. Adreena smiled to herself; she thought that maybe Viola Smith had been on that team. After the teacher finished making seating arrangements, Adreena went up to front to ask Mrs. Mulligan about the picture she had noticed on the wall.

Mrs. Mulligan asked Adreena, "What is it?" Adreena asked what year the picture had been taken. Mrs. Mulligan told her 1936. Adreena wondered if Viola had played for that team. Adreena wanted to ask Mrs. Mulligan more about the picture on the wall, but she thought because it was the first day of school that it wouldn't be a good idea. Mrs. Mulligan started teaching her class.

At the end of class, the bell rang, and all of the students got up to leave. As they were leaving, Mrs. Mulligan told Adreena that she wanted to talk with her about the picture of the softball team she had seen on the wall. But before Mrs. Mulligan could start talking to Adreena, there was a knock on the door.

Mrs. Mulligan said, "Who's there?" It was Paula, and she asked Mrs. Mulligan if Adreena was there. Mrs. Mulligan said yes. Adreena came to the door and asked Paula, "What is it?" Paula told Adreena, "Your mother is waiting outside." Adreena asked Paula to tell her mother that she would be right out. Mrs. Mulligan told Adreena that, if she had to leave, that was okay. "We can continue with our talk tomorrow after class."

Adreena walked out to the area where her mother was and got into the car. As they were driving home, Mrs. Jones asked Adreena, "How was the first day of high school?" Adreena told her mother that school had been great that day. And then she said, "Mom, do you remember that book you and dad bought me when I was about ten years old?" Mrs. Jones said, "You mean the one about the softball player Viola Smith?"

With an excited voice, Adreena said, "Yes, that's the one! Well, Mom, I think the name of the team Viola played on is the Burnsfield Cats. My science teacher Mrs. Mulligan has a picture on her wall of a softball team called the Burnsfield Cats."

Mrs. Jones said, "Isn't that the same team Viola played on during her high school years?" Adreena told her mom she didn't really know, but she wasn't going to stop until she found out. Adreena and her mother finally made it home; Adreena couldn't wait to tell her dad the good news.

Mr. Jones wasn't home from work just yet, so Adreena started doing her homework. She knew that was one thing her parents were very serious about. And she knew doing her homework helped out a lot, especially when it came time to study for a test.

While Adreena is doing her homework someone opened up the door, singing. It was her dad. He asked her, "How was school?" She told him that it was okay. Then she said, "Dad, remember that book you and Mom bought me when I was about ten years old? About the softball player Viola Smith?" Mr. Jones said yes. Adreena said, "My science teacher Mrs. Mulligan has a picture of a softball team called the Burnsfield Cats. Dad, I think Viola might have been part of that team. The picture was taken in 1952." Mr. Jones replied, "Are you sure? There were a lot of teams back in those days."

Adreena told her father that she was almost sure that was the team Viola had played with. After Adreena finished her homework, she went upstairs to her bedroom. She wanted to clean up her room before dinner. After dinner Adreena was getting ready to go to bed, but before she did, she took her favorite book off the shelf and began reading it again from the place she had last stopped a while ago:

The score between Violas' team the Burnsfield Cats and the Dillon County Bears was still zero to zero. Neither team had scored yet. It was the bottom of the second inning. Hattie was the first to hit for the Burnsfield Cats. Hattie walked up to the plate with a worried look on her face. The pitcher for the Dillon County Bears was Cynthia Green, but she preferred to be called Cindy. And she was the type of pitcher who wasn't frightened of anything.

While standing in the batter's box, Hattie thought about what a student had told her about Cindy. One day she had been walking home from school and was passing through an alleyway she often used. Two dogs came out from behind a tall fence. Cindy stared both of them right in the face, and the dogs stopped barking and then turned around and ran away as fast as they could.

Hattie knew she had a job to do because Cindy didn't care. Cindy started warming up; she threw about three balls to her team's catcher, Windy Wire. She was one of the best catchers in the league. Windy asked Cindy if she was ready. Cindy yelled back, "Yes, I'm ready!"

Hattie dug deep into the batter's box. Coach Melvin yelled out to Hattie, "Just play ball!" Cindy threw her first ball to Hattie; she missed. The umpire yelled, "Strike one!" Hattie started shaking her head back and forth because the pressure of facing Cindy was starting to get to her. Coach Melvin told Hattie, "Don't let her bother you." Hattie said to herself, "Coach, you don't see what I'm seeing." Cindy didn't have a smile on her face at all; she meant business. Cindy cleared the red dirt off the pitcher's mound. She wanted to make sure her pitches counted.

Then Cindy threw the ball to Hattie again, and it came hard. Hattie swung, and she missed. The umpire yelled, "Strike two!" Hattie looked worried. Coach Melvin called time out. He walked over to Hattie and told her to just try to hit the ball and keep her head up. Coach Melvin walked back to the dugout, and Viola asked Coach Melvin, "Is Hattie okay?" Coach Melvin said, "Yes, she's just a little scared, but I believe she's going to hit this next ball."

Cindy looked over at her coach, Queenie Jameson; she smiled back at Cindy and then nodded her head. Cindy knew what had to be done. Cindy pitched the ball again to Hattie, and it came even faster this time. Hattie stepped up and swung really hard; but she missed the ball, and the umpire yelled, "Strike three! You're out!" Cindy's teammates and all the parents clapped for her.

Hattie walked into the dugout with her head down. She looked at Viola and said, "I tried, I tried. I swear, Viola, I tried." Viola told Hattie, "Don't worry—the score is still zero to zero. It's Lucy's turn to hit." Before Lucy left the dugout she told Coach Melvin, "Don't worry. I'll hit the ball." Coach Melvin said, "Just do your best, and let the ball come to you."

Lucy was ready to hit. The umpire yelled, "Batter up!" Coach Queenie whispered something into Cindy's ear and headed back to the dugout. Cindy threw her first pitch. Lucy hit the ball, but it went foul. The umpire yelled, "Foul ball!" Lucy smiled from ear to ear because she had hit the ball just like she had said she would. The Cats were jumping up and down and yelling.

The umpire yelled, "Play ball!" Cindy threw another pitch. Lucy hit the ball again, and this time it went to right field, straight over the head of the Bears first baseman, Helen Mayfield. Lucy started running to first base, and she made it. The Cats were going crazy; Coach Melvin took his hat off and threw it up in the air. Lucy yelled back to her team in the dugout, "Come on, girls, we can do this!"

Cindy was really mad; you can practically see smoke coming out of her ears. The umpire looked at Coach Melvin and said, "Coach, send your next batter out." It was Viola's turn to bat next. Lucy yelled from first base, "Bring me home, Viola! Bring me home!" Viola looks at her and said, "Okay, get ready … I'm going to bring you home, girl!" Cindy still had that angry look on her face.

Coach Queenie didn't think Viola would stand a chance against Cindy's quick pitching. Cindy threw her first pitch to Viola, who missed it. The umpire yelled, "Strike one!" Everyone in the Bears dugout was yelling and jumping up and down. Viola shook her head. She knew that this was going to be tough, but she stayed focused.

Cindy walked with Helen and gave her a handshake. Viola yelled out to them, "I wouldn't celebrate just yet if I were you." Cindy said, "Oh yeah?" Then Cindy threw the second pitch; Viola stepped back, swung again, and missed. The Bears were screaming and cheering really loud. Coach Queenie yelled out very loudly to Cindy, "One more time!" Coach Melvin was nervous, and he was sweating so bad, you could squeeze water out of his shirt. Coach Queenie called time out.

The umpire yelled, "Time out, Bears!" Then Coach Queenie walked out to the pitcher's mound and told Cindy to just relax and take her time. "You can do it," she said. Lucy was yelling, "I know you're ready, Viola! Bring me home!" The umpire yelled, "Play ball!" Cindy wiped the sweat off her head, and she stared Viola right in the eyes. Wendy was giving Cindy all kinds of signals as to what kind of pitch to throw next to Viola.

Cindy finally chose a signal to throw. Then Cindy threw the third pitch. Viola stepped to the front of the batter's box. She hit the ball, and it went out and over the center fielder's head. Cindy yelled out to the outfield, "Throw it in!" Lucy ran to second base and then to third. She made it home, scoring one run for he team. Coach Melvin was yelling, "Come on, Viola!"

Viola rounded the bases. The ball was thrown from the outfield and in to Wendy, the catcher; but before Wendy could get to the ball, Viola made it across home plate. Viola walked into the dugout, the team was cheering and calling her name, "Viola! Viola!" The score was now two to zero. The Burnsfield Cats were in the lead. Another one of the umpires called a time out; he said, "I need to talk with the teams' coaches." He signaled to them to meet him in the field by the pitcher's mound. The coaches walked over to the umpire.

He said, "My name is Cab Jenkins. I am the head umpire here, and I called you over here because I need all of you to turn around and look at that dark cloud in the sky." Coach Queenie said, "Yes, it looks like it's getting ready to storm." Coach Melvin agreed and he said, "It looks like it is going to rain hard." Then Umpire Cab looked at them and said, "I need you to keep an eye on the weather. Because if it starts to rain even a little bit, I'm going to call the game, are we clear on that?" They all agreed. Then Umpire Cab said, "We are going to pick up where we left off. But let me remind you, if I feel a drop of rain, the game is over." The coaches nodded their heads and said okay.

And then the coaches walked back to their dugouts and explained to their players what they had talked about with Umpire Cab. Viola asked Coach Melvin if she could talk with the team. He said, "Sure, Viola." Viola told the team, "We need to score a few more runs, and we've got to beat this team ... Remember, they beat us last year." Coach Melvin explained to the girls that Umpire Cab had said that if he felt the first sign of rain, he was going to call the game. "So, we have to make every hit count."

Coach Melvin then told the girls, "On the count of three, let's all yell 'Finish!' really loud. One, two, three, finish!" The Cats knew what they had to do. They didn't want this team to come back and beat them under any circumstances. The Burnsfield Cats were about to start hitting again, but just as Thelma walked up to the batter's box to hit, it started raining.

Coach Melvin called the team together, but before he could start talking, Umpire Cab called Coach Queenie and Coach Melvin out onto the field again. He told both of them that the game was over because of the rain. Umpire Cab said, "That means the Burnsfield Cats win, because they have already scored two runs in the game."

Coach Melvin walked back to the dugout and told the team the news. Viola yelled out, "I can't believe it! We finally beat the Dillon County Bears!" The entire Burnsfield Cats team jumped up and started yelling; they were extremely happy about the win.

While the Burnsfield Cats were celebrating their win, Lucy noticed that Margret Filmner had started walking towards them. Lucy started calling out, "Viola! Viola! Viola!" And Viola turned around and said, "What, Lucy?" Lucy said, "Look!" Viola said, "Oh, boy!" Lucy asked Viola, "What are we going to do?" Then Viola said, "What do you mean? What are we going to do?" As Margret walked up to the dugout, everyone got quiet.

Coach Melvin asked Margret, "Can I help you?" Margret pushed Coach Melvin aside and said in a stern voice to Viola, "You got lucky this time ... but we will meet again, and I will be ready to pay you back." Then Margret turned around and left. The girls looked at each other; they knew Margret meant what she had said. Coach Melvin looked at Lucy and Viola with a confused look on his face. Coach Melvin asked the girls, "Who was that? And what was that all about?" Both Viola and Lucy told Coach Melvin, "She goes to Burnsfield Middle School also. And that one morning at school when we were outside playing a game of softball, Viola struck Margret out just before the bell rang to go inside."

Coach Melvin said, "And what was so bad about that?" Lucy replied, "We only had about three seconds left to play, and Viola threw the last ball the same time the bell rang and struck her out. Margret was embarrassed." Then Viola said, "Coach, she's been mad with me since then." Coach Melvin sat down, took his hat off, grabbed his handkerchief from his back pocket, and wiped the sweat from his head with it. He had a bewildered look on his face as he thought about what the girls had just told him. Coach Melvin had thought Margret was an adult because Margret was a big girl and she looked a lot older than a middle school student would look. They all pulled themselves together and picked up their equipment and left the dugout.

The weather was starting to get bad. Coach Melvin told the girls that he would call them and let them know when their next game would be; he also told them to make sure they did their schoolwork and kept their grades up.

Adreena fell asleep while reading her favorite book. Mr. Jones was getting ready to go to bed, and he decided to look in on Adreena. When he saw that she had fallen asleep, he walked over to her bed to make sure she was comfortable. He had noticed that she had been reading the book about her favorite softball player. Mr. Jones just knew that one day his daughter was going to become a professional softball player.

Mr. Jones turned the light off and closed the door to Adreena's room. He walked back to his bedroom, and Mrs. Jones asked, "What's wrong, Bryan?" He just laughed and said, "Mary, I believe we have a very special ball player on our hands."

Mrs. Jones said, "Yes, she is determined to play softball." The next morning came around and Mr. and Mrs. Jones got ready for work. Mrs. Jones asked Mr. Jones to check on Adreena to see if she was getting ready also so she could be dropped off at school. Mr. Jones knocked on Adreena's bedroom door, but she didn't answer. Mr. Jones yelled, "Adreena!" She called out, "Yes, Dad?" Mr. Jones said, "Adreena, where are you, dear?" Adreena answered, "Downstairs, eating breakfast!" Mr. Jones asked, "Adreena, what time did you get up this morning?" Adreena told her dad, "About 6:30. I was hungry, and I couldn't wait."

Mr. Jones said to Adreena, "Okay, honey, you have a good day at school." Then Mr. Jones left for work, and Mrs. Jones and Adreena headed out the door too. Mrs. Jones dropped Adreena off at school, and then she went to work. Adreena started walking toward her class, and two girls walked up beside her. Their names were Janice Marks and Pepper Thomas, and they started making fun of Adreena's clothes.

Pepper said, "Well, well, what do we have here? She's dressed like a little candy cane for the merry holidays." Then Janice and Pepper grabbed Adreena's purse and tried to open it. As they were doing that, two more girls walked up beside them: Candy Walker and Keisha Brown. They asked, "What's going on here? Why are you two picking on her and going through her purse?" Then Pepper and Janice looked at each other like they knew they were in trouble; Candy and Keisha were much bigger and taller than they were.

Candy and Keisha suggested to Janice and Pepper that they give Adreena her purse back and leave before trouble started for them. When Pepper and Janice left, Candy and Keisha turned and looked at

Adreena. They said to her, "Girl, you don't know who we are?" Adreena looked at them, still unsure, and then she said, "Candy? Candy Walker? And Keisha ... Brown? You mean both of you go to school here too?"

Both Candy and Keisha answered at the same time, "Yeah, girl!" Adreena said, "I am so glad the two of you showed up when you did because I was about to get seriously hurt by those two girls." Adreena then said to Candy and Keisha, "You will not believe who else goes to school here from the old team." They said, "Who?" Adreena said, "Paula," and both Keisha and Candy started laughing. Keisha said, "You mean Paula Jackson? I guarantee she is somewhere telling jokes." They all started laughing. The bell rang; it was time for Adreena, Candy, and Keisha to get to their classes. When Adreena's first period was over with, she decided to go to the library and do some work instead of going to lunch. The librarian came by the table where Adreena was sitting and introduced herself to Adreena. She said, "My name is Mrs. Mable Green."

Adreena noticed that Mrs. Green was wearing a sweater with writing on it that read, "Burnsfield Cats High School Softball Team, Class of 1936." Adreena wanted to ask Mrs. Green if she knew a player by the name of Viola Smith. She did not have time, though, since she was trying to get her work done before her next class. Adreena was working hard on her papers. Coach Lawson walked into the library and noticed Adreena sitting at the table. So he walked over and asked her, "What are you doing here?" Adreena said, "I am going over some papers I need for history, which is my next class."

Mrs. Green, the librarian, came over to ask Coach Lawson if he needed help with anything. Coach told her, "No, everything is alright." Then Coach Lawson told Adreena and Mrs. Green that he had to leave and go back to class. Adreena also had to leave, so she wouldn't be late getting to her history class. As Adreena was leaving the library, she ran into Paula, and Paula asked, "Adreena, are you okay?" Adreena says yes. Then Paula said, "I heard about what happened earlier with you and those girls. You know, that didn't make any sense at all." Adreena stayed quiet.

Paula thought maybe telling a joke would cheer her up. So Paula asked Adreena, "What president wore the tallest hat?" Adreena asked Paula, "What are you talking about, girl?" "Come on, Adreena, just answer the question. What president wore the tallest hat?" Adreena said, "Okay, okay. Paula, I don't know … Which one?" Paula told her that she didn't know either. Adreena looked at Paula and said, "Girl, you're so crazy." And they both looked at each other and started laughing.

Adreena and Paula then went their separate ways. Adreena walked into her history class, and she noticed a Burnsfield Cats banner on the wall over the clock. Adreena was becoming more and more curious; it seemed like all of her teachers had something to do with the softball team she thought Viola had played on.

But Adreena didn't know if she was just so caught up and into Viola's story and the love of the game of softball that her imagination was taking over and playing tricks on her. But Adreena still wanted to ask her history teacher, Mrs. Lucy White, a question about the Burnsfield Cats Softball Team. She knew her class work was more important, though, so she just went to her seat and sat down.

Mrs. White asked everyone to take out their history books and turn to page twelve. She said that the first chapter was on Civil Rights. "And you're going to have a test in a week on this chapter," She added. Mrs. White asked if anyone would like to read first, but none of the students raised their hands.

So Mrs. White chose Adreena and asked her to please read the first paragraph. Adreena said, "Okay, Mrs. White." And as Adreena was reading, Mrs. White said, "It is getting cold in here." She walked around to the back of her desk to get to her chair, which had a sweater hanging on the back of it. She picked up the sweater and put it on.

Adreena was still reading, but she seemed to be having some trouble with one of the words in the paragraph. Mrs. White asked Adreena,

"What's wrong? Do you need help with that word?" Adreena said yes, and Mrs. White said, "Take your time, Adreena, and pronounce the word slowly. That will help you say it right."

Adreena looked up at Mrs. White and noticed she had the same sweater on as Mrs. Green, the librarian: "Burnsfield Cats High School Softball Team, Class of 1952." Adreena started shaking her head; she did not know what to think. Mrs. White asked Adreena, "Is everything alright?"

Adreena said yes. So Mrs. White pronounced the word Adreena had stumbled over and asked, "What is the word?" Adreena said, "The word is *arbitrary*." "Very good, Adreena," said Mrs. White. Adreena continued to read. She finished the first paragraph, and then Mrs. White reminded the class that the chapter would be on their test next week. Adreena knew she had a lot of studying and work to do before she took the test.

The bell rang, and Adreena headed to her math class. As soon as she walked out of Mrs. White's class, she ran into Coach Lawson again. He stopped Adreena in the hallway to let her know that there would be softball tryouts after school. Adreena told Coach Lawson that she would be there. Coach Lawson began to walk away, but then Adreena yelled out, "Coach Lawson, my equipment is at home!" He said, "That's okay. All you're going to do is hit the ball today. And I have equipment you can use." Then Coach Lawson told Adreena that he would be doing the pitching. "So, you don't have to worry about having your own equipment today." Adreena yelled back, "Okay, Coach Lawson! See you after school!"

After Adreena finished talking with Coach Lawson, she turned around, and Paula yelled, "Boo!" Adreena screamed and covered her mouth. Then she said, "Paula, when are you going to stop playing around?" Paula said, "I don't know, girl … Maybe when we finish school? You know me." Adreena and Paula went on to their next class. Adreena was excited about the softball tryouts.

Adreena finished the rest of her classes. And when school was finally over for the day, Adreena called her mom to let her know that she was staying after school for softball tryouts and that she would give her a call when it was over so she could pick her up. Then Adreena went to the girls' locker room to change for practice. She heard some girls laughing really loudly.

When Adreena turned the corner, there was Paula, sitting on the bench and talking with some girls who had just finished P.E. Adreena said, "Paula, I thought you said that you weren't going to tryout for the team." Paula said, "Well, Adreena, I thought I would give it another try. And, girl, you know I couldn't leave you hanging all by your lonesome." Then Paula nudged Adreena in the arm, smiled, and said, "Someone has to listen to my jokes." Adreena looked at Paula, and then shook her head and laughed.

While Adreena was changing into her practice clothes, she heard more girls talking. Then she turned around and saw Candy and Keisha. She asked them, "What are you two doing here?" Both Candy and Keisha told Adreena, "Girl, we could not let you have all of the fun. And besides, we make a good team." Then Coach Lawson started blowing his whistle to get the girls' attention so they would come outside and meet him at the school's softball field.

The girls arrived at the softball field where Coach Lawson was waiting for them. Coach Lawson asked all of the girls to sit down in the bleachers. He said, "I need to point out a few things to you. Everyone will have a fair chance to become a part of this team, but I can only pick fifteen players to be on the team. So just do your best. I feel like this is going to be a good season."

Coach Lawson asked the girls, "Does anyone have any questions?" Adreena raised her hand. Coach Lawson said, "Yes, what is it?" Adreena asked, "Coach, how many games are we going to play this year?" Coach Lawson says, "Well, Adreena, we're going to play at least fifteen games this year." Then Adreena asked Coach Lawson, "Will we be playing any teams from Dillon County?" Coach Lawson answered, "Yes, we will!" After that answer, Adreena said, "Oh, boy!" She got a worried look on her face.

After Coach Lawson finished talking to the girls, he said, "Now, everyone, I would like to introduce you to my assistant, Coach Connie Smith." Then Coach Lawson told the girls that Coach Connie has been teaching at the school for quite some time. Everyone said hello to Coach Connie. And Coach Connie looked at the girls with a big smile on her face. Keisha asked Coach Connie, "Have you always taught school here?" Coach Connie answered, "Yes, Keisha, I have." Then Coach Connie said to the girls, "Since I'm already answering your questions about me. Let me just tell you a little bit more about myself. I was born here in Montiville in March of 1954. I went to the old Montiville High School before they built this new school. I played softball there for about three years, and then I also played softball in college. I went to Newt Brimmery College in West Virginia. I graduated in 1974 with a master's degree in teaching.

While Coach Connie was talking, Candy told some of the girls that Coach Connie seemed to be a really nice person—but, boy! She could yell really loud! Candy said, "I remember there was one time when I was walking down the hallway, and I heard Coach Connie yelling at the class about something." Adreena asked, "Candy, are you sure?" Candy said yes. Coach Connie finished talking to the girls, and then Coach Lawson told all the girls to walk over to the auditorium where they would watch some films about softball. Adreena asked Coach Lawson, "Will this help us out?" Coach Lawson replied, "More than you know." Everyone made it to the auditorium and took a seat. Coach Lawson suggested that everyone get comfortable and pay attention to the films.

All of the other players were taking out pencils and papers to take notes during the film. Coach Lawson told the players that this film was about the techniques of softball and how to use them. Adreena thought she would take a seat in the back under the soft lighting so she could watch the film and be able to read more about the one and only softball player she wanted to be like. She began to read:

Viola got home from the game and finished her homework. And after the rain and bad weather was over with, she told her mother that she was going outside to play. While she was outside playing, Viola heard the loud noise of someone yelling. Viola told her mom that she would be right back. She noticed some kids standing down the street looking over an old broken fence. Viola asked them, "What are you looking at?" And Turner Palmer, who lived just a couple of houses down from Viola, said, "A lady coach, and she is coaching a men's baseball team."

Viola asked Turner, "Is she the one doing all the yelling?" Turner said, "Yes, that's her." Viola told Turner, "You know, yelling at those players isn't going to do anything but make them mad." Turner said, "You're right, Viola." Then Turner said, "Viola, why don't we just leave?" Turner knew how Viola's attitude was and that she didn't mind speaking up—especially about unfairness.

Turner knew Viola was about to say something. He tried to get her to leave with him by saying, "There isn't anything that we can do about it." But Viola looked through the broken fence again. The coach got louder and louder with her yelling and putting her players down. And the players were practicing as hard as they could. The first baseman dropped the ball every time the pitcher threw it to him. And the coach would yell, "Hey! What are you doing? You couldn't catch a cold if you wanted to!" Then the first baseman would drop his head in disbelief that his coach was saying that to him. Viola told Turner, "She seems really mean."

The coach called all the players together and told them in a loud voice, "If you do not want to practice, then please go home!" Viola looked at Turner, and Turner said, "What's wrong Viola? You've got that look in your eyes. What are you going to do?" "I'm going to tell that coach if she stops yelling at them they might practice a whole lot better." Turner started pleading with Viola, "Don't do that. Please, Viola! You don't know what you're getting yourself into." Viola told Turner in an angry voice, "I don't care—she shouldn't treat her players that way!"

Viola jumped over the old, broken wooden fence. She walked across the field toward the coach, who was standing outside of the dugout. Viola yelled out, "Hey, you!" The coach turned and looked at Viola and said, "What are you doing? You could get hit by one of these baseballs." Then she asked Viola, "Who told you to climb over that broken fence? You could get hurt really bad doing that."

Then the coach said, "So, what can I do for you, young lady?" Viola said, "Well, Coach … uh … uh." Viola sounded like she was getting ready to lose her voice. Turner couldn't believe what Viola had gotten herself into. So Turner thought he would call Viola's name a few times: "Viola! Viola! VIOLA!" And she yelled back to him, "Are you trying to serenade me? Or trying to get my attention?" Viola put her hand up, waved, and yelled to Turner, "Be quiet!"

Then Viola told the coach, "You know, if you would stop yelling at your players, they might play better for you." The coach asked Viola, "Was I yelling that loud?" Viola said, "Yes, I could hear you down the road where I live." Then the coach said to Viola in a harsh tone, "Oh, yeah? And what do you want me to do about it?" Viola said, "Well, Coach, you could stop yelling at them. That only makes them nervous and not want to play like they're supposed to." The Coach asked Viola, "Do you play softball?" Viola said, "Yes, I do." The coach then said, "Well, what position do you play?" Viola said to the coach, "I'm a pitcher."

The coach said, "A pitcher, really?" So the Coach decided to make a bet with Viola. She said to Viola, "If you can strike out two of my best hitters, I will stop yelling at my players." Then Viola says, "But I pitch for a softball team." The coach then said, "Viola, do you fast pitch in softball?" Viola said yes, and the coach replied, "Well, then that shouldn't be a problem, right?" Viola had a worried look on her face; she thought that maybe she had bitten off more than she could chew.

Then the Coach asked Viola in a sarcastic tone, "Are you ready, or not?" Viola tried not to look nervous and said, "Sure, Coach, I'm ready. Let's get started." The coach then told one of her players to let Viola use one of their gloves to pitch with. Then the first player stepped up into the batter's box. He said to Viola, "Hey, little lady, they call me 'Slammer,'" Viola mumbled to herself, "This should be a lot of fun."

Then Viola stepped back and dug her feet into the pitcher's mound and threw her first pitch. Slammer grabbed hold of the bat tightly, swung, and hit the ball—but it went foul. He looked over at his coach, and she yelled out to him, "Pay attention!" Slammer dropped his head with a discouraged look on his face. And Viola just shook her head from side to side and said to herself, "I can't believe this coach." Then Viola's friend Turner yelled across the fence, "Come on, Viola! You can do it!" Viola's mom, dad, and some of the other neighbors started showing up to see what was going on, and they all were lined up along the broken fence.

Everyone was cheering Viola on. She looked over at the crowd and was amazed at how many people were there cheering for her. Viola was getting ready to throw her second ball, and then someone in the crowd yelled, "Remember, what I showed you!" She looked around and saw that it was her brother Demi. He had a big smile on his face. Viola stepped up to the plate again; she knew that Slammer could get another lucky hit, so she had to make this second pitch count. Viola took her glove off and rubbed the back of her hand across her face. Demi yelled out to Viola, "Are you okay?" Viola looked at Demi and nodded her head yes and gave him a big smile. Demi knew what was getting ready to happen next.

Viola put her glove back on her hand and stared straight at Slammer with a mean look on her face. Then Viola threw her second pitch. The ball was coming fast, and Slammer's eyes got big. As the ball came across the plate, he tried to hit it as hard as he could. But Viola had thrown him a strike. Slammer had really thought he was going to hit the ball. Then Slammer looked over at his coach, and she yelled, "What are you looking at? Am I going to have to hit the ball for you, too?" Slammer just dropped his head in embarrassment. Viola didn't want to pitch to Slammer anymore, but she had to show the coach that she could strike out her two best players. And she also wanted to show the coach that she could pitch. Viola knew that this was the only way she could get the coach's attention and get her to stop yelling at her players.

Viola had a handkerchief in her pants pocket, so she used it to take the orange clay off the pitcher's mound. When Viola finished cleaning off the mound, she turned around slowly and looked over at her mother and brother. She grabbed the ball and started blowing the dust off. Then Viola took two big deep breaths. And then Viola stepped back and threw her third ball. Slammer's knees were shaking uncontrollably.

The ball came flying across home plate. Slammer did all he could to hit the ball, but he missed. Slammer was hesitant to look over at his coach again, but he did. And she yelled out really loudly, "Slammer, I can't believe it! You're good for nothing!" Slammer just looked away from her and walked into the dugout. Viola shook her head in disbelief at how the coach was putting Slammer down. Then Viola looked around and saw that she had half of the neighborhood cheering her on. The coach looked at Viola and said, "You have one more batter." The second batter that came out of the dugout was Slammer Jenkins's twin brother, Jammer Jenkins.

Before Jammer went out to the batter's box, his coach wanted to talk with him. She yelled at him in a nasty tone, "Jammer, you'd better not miss, or you will be our new bat boy!" Jammer told his coach, "I'll do my best," and the coach yelled back, "Jammer, I do not want your best—I want you to hit the ball, okay?"

Viola couldn't believe what she was hearing. She said to herself, "I have to make this work." Viola was getting ready to throw the ball, but she noticed that her shoelaces were coming untied, so she stopped and tied them. After she'd finished tying her shoes, Viola looked up at the next batter with a puzzled look on her face. She said to herself, "I know

A PITCHER TO REMEMBER

it's hot out here, but I can't believe it. Am I seeing double, or are my eyes playing tricks on me?" Viola was right; she was seeing double: it was Slammer's twin brother, Jammer, batting next.

Jammer yelled out to Viola, "Today just isn't going to be your day!" Viola just looked back at Jammer with a big smile on her face. Jammer had no idea what he was about to get himself into. Viola got ready to step up to the plate to throw the ball, but she stopped, looked at Jammer, and said, "What is he doing?" Jammer had bowed his head and was praying.

After Jammer had finished praying, he was ready to try to hit anything and everything Viola threw at him. Viola stepped up to the plate and threw her first pitch to Jammer. He was so nervous, sweat was pouring off his head, like someone had poured a bucket of water on him. Jammer swung at the ball and missed.

The coach yelled at Jammer, "Remember, what I told you!" Jammer shook his head from side to side and stepped away from the batter's box. He was trying hard not to let the coach's words get to him. Jammer stepped back into the batter's box and got himself ready for the next pitch.

Viola then told Jammer, "Here comes the second pitch." By this time almost everyone from the neighborhood was watching Viola take on this baseball team's two best hitters. Some of her teammates are watching, and one of them yelled out, "You can do it, girl!"

Viola looked around quickly and saw that it was Lucy, the second baseman for their softball team. Viola threw the ball to Jammer, and he hit a foul ball. His coach yelled out, "Jammer, I'm warning you!" Viola said to herself, "Now it is time to seal the deal ... Sorry, Jammer, but this is for your own good." Viola didn't waste any time. She threw her third and final pitch to Jammer.

The coach yelled out, "Okay, Jammer, you better hit this ball!" The ball looked like it was coming to Jammer in slow motion; he swung hard and tried to hit it—but he missed. The crowd yelled "Alright! Good job,

Viola!" The coach and her team were shocked and could not believe what had just happened. Everyone was cheering Viola on because she had struck out the baseball team's two best hitters. The coach walked up to Viola and reached out to shake her hand.

The coach said, "Okay, kid, you've got yourself a deal. No more yelling at my players." Then the coach introduced herself to Viola. She said, "I'm Coach Bell Showers, and the name of this team is the Pembrook Pythons." Viola's mouth dropped, and her eyes got really big. She couldn't believe it: she was pitching against one of the best teams in the baseball league. Viola said to Coach Bell, "I've heard about this team." Then Viola asked Coach Bell, "How come you don't have the team's name on the back of their practice jerseys?" Coach Bell said, "Because of our popularity. I don't allow the players to wear any practice jerseys with the team's name on them. We come to Montville to practice, because it's a small town and we're not recognized here."

While Viola was talking with the coach, her brother Demi walked up. Viola introduced Demi to Coach Bell, and then the team's other coach came out of the dugout. He said, "You're Demi Smith, right?" Demi replied, "Yes, sir, I am." Then the coach said, "Hi, I'm Coach Less Payor. I recognized your face. Do you still pitch for the Georgia Hawks?" Demi answered, "Yes, sir, I still do." Coach Payor told Viola, "You're lucky to have a brother like him." Viola gave Demi a big hug with a big smile on her face and said, "I know."

Viola and Demi and their mom and dad started walking back home, and everyone was talking about what Viola had done. Then Viola stopped she said, "Wait a minute!" Demi asked, "What's wrong?" She said, "We forgot Turner." And as soon as she said that, Turner came running up to Viola. He said, "Viola, you're the best and also a little weird–but you're alright with me." Viola, Demi, Turner, and Viola's mom and dad made it back home. Viola told her parents that she was going to walk Turner back to his house, and Viola's mom said, "Make sure you hurry back. It's dinner time."

A PITCHER TO REMEMBER

After walking Turner home, Viola hurried back to her house to help set up the table for dinner. As they were preparing the table, someone knocked at the door. Viola, Demi, and Mr. Smith finished up setting the table while Mrs. Smith answered the door. It was Coach Bell. Mrs. Smith told her to come in.

When Viola, Demi, and Mr. Smith saw who it was at the door, they stopped setting the table and walked over toward the door. Then Coach Bell said, "I just wanted to let Viola know that she was right about how I was treating my players. No one has ever talked to me like that before; you have a lot of courage and spunk, young lady." Viola then said, "I didn't mean any disrespect toward you; I just thought you were being disrespectful to your players and that was unfair to them, so that's why I said something to you." Coach Bell said, "I got the message loud and clear."

Coach Bell had to leave, and as she was leaving she stopped, turned around, and then said to Viola, "I would like for you to play on my team someday." Viola said, "We'll see what the future holds," but she could hardly keep the excitement inside. After Coach Bell left, Viola's family told her that they were proud of her for speaking up for those players like she did. And her brother Demi said to her with a big grin on his face, "You seemed to have gotten a spot on a professional league waiting on you out of this whole ordeal." Viola just smiled. Then Mrs. Smith told Viola to go and change for dinner. So Viola went up to her bedroom to change, and all of a sudden she heard something hitting the window. It was Turner throwing rocks at her window. Viola came to the window, and Turner quickly closed his eyes.

Viola asked Turner, "Why do you have your eyes closed?" He said, "You're a girl, right?" Viola answered him in a laughing voice, "Yes, I am. But, Turner, I have my clothes on." Then Turner asked Viola, "So, I can open my eyes, right?" Still laughing, Viola said, "Turner, you're so silly. I thought I left you at home. So, what do you want?" Turner said, "I was thinking, if you had some time one day, could you teach me to pitch like you?" Viola said, "No problem; now go home before you get me in trouble!"

Adreena had to stop reading about Viola. The film was over. Coach Lawson told the girls that he was changing tryouts to the next day, and he wanted everyone to show up again after school. Coach Lawson then said to them, "We have a heavy playing schedule ahead of us. We're going to play some schools with players that can hit and have a lot of experience playing ball. So if you're serious about playing softball for the school, please show up and be on time for practice tomorrow."

Adreena felt good about playing softball for the school. And as she was walking back to the locker room to get her things, Coach Connie told her that she wanted to talk with her. Coach Connie said, "Adreena, I noticed while Coach Lawson was showing the film, you were reading a book and also watching the film." Then Coach Connie asked Adreena, "Could you tell me about the book you were reading?"

Adreena told her, "It was a book about a softball player that my mother gave to me when I was younger and started playing softball for the first time." Coach Connie asked Adreena, "Who was the player you were reading about?" Adreena said, "Her name is Viola Smith, and that lady was one heck of a softball player." Coach Connie turned away from Adreena for a few seconds with a smile on her face. Then Coach Connie told Adreena that she would like to read that book someday.

While Coach Connie and Adreena were talking, Paula walked up behind them, and she asked Adreena, "What are you going to do when you get home?" Adreena said, "I have a lot of homework to do." Then she asked Paula, "Do you have any homework?"

Paula said to Adreena, "Girl, are you crazy? That's like trying to tell the Joker in a Batman movie that he isn't funny. I completed all of my work in class." Coach Connie and Adreena shook their heads and started laughing. Adreena told Paula, "Girl, I believe you have lost it." Coach Connie continued to laugh, and she told Paula, "You certainly know how to keep people smiling."

Coach Connie told the girls that she would see them later. Adreena and Paula walked back to the locker room, and then they walked to the front of the school where their parents were waiting to pick them up. On the way home Adreena told her mom that she couldn't wait until they started playing against other teams. She said, "Coach Lawson showed us a film about some softball techniques."

Mrs. Jones told Adreena that she might need to put those techniques to use in her games. Adreena told her mom that she had learned a lot about playing softball. "And ever since you and Dad signed me up for softball, I have enjoyed every minute of it." Adreena asked her mom if she had ever played softball. And her mom replied, "Yes, I did." Adreena asked her mom, "Who did you play for?" Mrs. Jones told her that she had played for a team in school up north. Adreena looked at her mom with a big smile on her face. When her mom said that Adreena knew then why she liked softball so much.

Adreena and her mother arrived home, and her father was sitting in his favorite chair watching TV. When Adreena walked through the door, her father asked her, "How was her day?" Adreena told her dad that they had watched a film in practice about softball techniques, and with excitement Adreena said, "Dad, guess what? It was okay—I learned a lot." After telling her father about the film, Adreena decided that she would go upstairs and do her homework.

Mrs. Jones sat down next to Mr. Jones and told him that Adreena had asked her if she had played softball before and for what school. Mrs. Jones said, "I told her yes and that I played for a school up north." Mr. Jones started to laugh and wondered why Adreena was asking a lot of questions. "And what is on that little lady's mind?" With a smile on her face, Mrs. Jones said to Mr. Jones, "I couldn't tell you, honey." She went to go get dinner started and left Mr. Jones in the den watching TV.

But before starting dinner, Mrs. Jones wanted to check in on Adreena. So she went upstairs and knocked on Adreena's bedroom door. Adreena asked, "Who is it?" Mrs. Jones answered, "It's me, honey."

Adreena said, "Come in." Mrs. Jones entered and asked Adreena, "And how is school?" Adreena said, "It's going okay." And then Mrs. Jones asked, "Adreena, are you still reading that book I got for you when you first started playing softball?" Adreena answered, "Yes, I still have it, and I keep it with me in my book bag. I'm almost finished reading it." Mrs. Jones was very surprised but pleased to hear all of this.

After Mrs. Jones finished talking with Adreena, she walked back downstairs to get dinner started. And as Mrs. Jones was getting dinner ready, there was a knock at the door. Both Mr. and Mrs. Jones went to the door to see who was there. It was Mrs. Zipperman; she was the kind of lady who was always in a good mood. Nothing seemed to ever make her mad or get her down. Mr. and Mrs. Jones told her to come in, and as Mrs. Zipperman walked in, Mrs. Jones asked her how she was doing. Mrs. Zipperman said, "I am doing okay." Then Mr. Jones asked her, "What can we help you with this evening?"

Mrs. Zipperman said that she was getting ready to bake a cake and that she needed a couple of eggs. Mrs. Jones told Mrs. Zipperman that she only had a few eggs left, but Mrs. Zipperman said that she only needed three eggs. Mrs. Jones went to the kitchen to get the eggs for her. By this time Adreena was headed downstairs, and she saw Mrs. Zipperman. Adreena said, "Hi, Mrs. Zipperman. What brings you over?" She told Adreena that she was getting ready to bake a cake and needed some eggs.

Then Adreena asked Mrs. Zipperman, "Is it your birthday today?" Mrs. Zipperman said, "No, it's my granddaughter's birthday." Adreena asked, "Who is your granddaughter?" Mrs. Zipperman told her that her granddaughter's name was Eloise Filmner. Adreena thought to herself that she had heard that name somewhere before. Adreena ran back upstairs to find her book about Viola Smith. She looked in her book bag, and there it was. Adreena picked the book up and turned a few pages, and there was the name Margret Filmner. Adreena remembered reading about how mean Margret was to Viola. And she also remembered how tough Margret Filmner was and that everyone was scared of her.

Adreena dropped the book back into the book bag and covered her mouth in surprise, because of what she had just discovered. Then she ran back downstairs. Adreena stopped and stared straight at Mrs. Zipperman with her eyes opened really big. Mrs. Jones asked, "Adreena, are you okay?" She said, "Uh, yes, Mom. I'm okay." Then Adreena asked Mrs. Zipperman, "How old will your granddaughter be?" She said, "She will be turning fifty years old today." Mrs. Zipperman asked Adreena if she wanted to meet her granddaughter.

At first Adreena didn't answer. She had a blank look on her face. Mrs. Zipperman asked her again, "Adreena do you want to meet her?" Again, Adreena said nothing. Mrs. Jones said, "Adreena, don't you hear Mrs. Zipperman talking to you?" And in a shaky voice Adreena said, "Yes, Mom, I hear Mrs. Zipperman talking to me." Mrs. Jones said, "Well, are you going to answer her?" Adreena finally got over being scared and told Mrs. Zipperman, "Yes, I would like to meet your granddaughter." Mr. Jones asked Adreena, "Are you okay?" She said, "Uh, yes, Dad. I'm okay." Adreena then turned around and walked back upstairs to her room.

Mrs. Jones gave Mrs. Zipperman the eggs she needed and told Mrs. Zipperman she didn't know what was wrong with Adreena but that she would find out. Mrs. Zipperman then said, "When my granddaughter arrives from out of town, I will bring her over and introduce you to her." Mrs. Jones said, "Okay, we would love to meet her." Mrs. Zipperman said, "Okay, and thank you so much for these eggs … Now I can bake that cake."

When Mrs. Zipperman left, Mrs. Jones walked into the kitchen to check on dinner. Mr. Jones told Mrs. Jones that he would go upstairs and check on Adreena. So he went upstairs and asked Adreena, "What was going on with you downstairs, young lady? You were acting as if you had seen a ghost." Adreena said, "Dad, it's nothing. I was just overreacting." Adreena didn't want to tell her father why she was really acting the way she was. All she knew was that she kind of felt like Viola did when it came to Margret Filmner.

And even though it was just Mrs. Zipperman's granddaughter, Adreena just didn't want to face her. Mr. Jones told Adreena, "If you need to talk to your mother and me, we are here for you, okay?" Adreena said, "Okay, Dad." Mr. Jones then reached over and gave her a kiss on the forehead. Then he left and went back downstairs. Mrs. Jones asked him, "Was everything okay?" And Mr. Jones replied, "She's okay, honey. I guess she was just a little on the tired side. You know she has been doing a lot of homework and getting herself ready to play on the softball team for her school, and that's been a lot of pressure on her." Mrs. Jones said, "I guess you're right, honey." And then she said, "Dinner will be ready in about ten minutes."

Mr. Jones went back to sit in his favorite chair and started watching TV again. The phone rang, and Mrs. Jones answered it. It was Mrs. Zipperman; she told Mrs. Jones that her granddaughter had just arrived from out of town and that she would be bringing her over in a few minutes. Mrs. Jones said, "That's good, Mrs. Zipperman. I will let Adreena know that you are on your way."

Mrs. Jones called to Adreena from downstairs, "Adreena! Adreena!" And then Adreena yelled out, "Yes, Mother!" Mrs. Jones said, "Could you please come down here?" Adreena said, "What is it, Mom?" "Mrs. Zipperman just called, and she said her granddaughter is here. She'll be bringing her over in a few minutes, and they may be staying for dinner."

Adreena just stayed quiet and tried to calm her nerves. She kept on repeating to herself, "Everything will be okay, everything will be okay." She thought about maybe asking her mom if it would be okay to invite Paula over for dinner to sort of smooth things out and help calm her nerves.

Adreena just did not know what to expect from Mrs. Zipperman's granddaughter, Eloise Filmner. By the time Mrs. Jones finished cooking dinner, Mrs. Zipperman and her granddaughter hadn't made it over yet, so Mrs. Jones called Mrs. Zipperman and told her to come on over and have dinner with them.

Mrs. Zipperman said, "Okay, we'll be right over." Adreena was setting the table, and her mom told her that Mrs. Zipperman would be there shortly. A few minutes later, there was a knock at the door, and her dad answered it. Mr. Jones told Mrs. Zipperman and her granddaughter to come on in. Then Mrs. Zipperman said to Mr. and Mrs. Jones, "This is my granddaughter, Eloise Filmner. She is from out of town." Eloise said to the Jones, "It's nice to meet you." Then Mrs. Zipperman asked, "Where is Adreena?" Mrs. Jones said, "She must be in the kitchen."

Mrs. Jones asked Adreena to come out into the living room and meet Mrs. Zipperman's granddaughter. When Adreena walked out of the kitchen, she stopped dead in her tracks and looked up at Eloise. She couldn't believe how tall Eloise was. Eloise asked Adreena, "How are you doing?" And nervously, Adreena said, "Well, uh, uh, okay."

Everyone went to the table and sat down for dinner. Mr. and Mrs. Jones sat at opposite ends of the table; Mrs. Zipperman sat on one side of Mr. Jones, and Eloise sat on the other side of Mr. Jones. Adreena sat by her mother, on the same side as Eloise. They started eating and talking, and the door bell rang. Mrs. Jones got up from the table to see who was at the door. It was Paula.

Mrs. Jones asked Paula, "Where is your mother and father?" Paula said, "They are on their way to a dinner party for my father's job, so I asked my mom to drop me off over here." Mrs. Jones said, "Paula, do you think you should have called first?" Paula said, "Well, Mrs. Jones, I figured since I was like family, it was okay to just come on over." Mrs. Jones just looked at Paula, shook her head, and smiled.

Then Adreena ran up to the door, grabbed Paula by the hand, and pulled her through the door. Paula sat across from Adreena, and Adreena offered Paula something to eat. Adreena then introduced Paula to Mrs. Zipperman and her granddaughter. While they were eating, Eloise asked Mrs. Jones, "Where is the bathroom?" She told Eloise, "It's down the hallway, to the right."

When Eloise got up from the table, Paula looked at Adreena and then she said to Eloise, "You must have ostrich in your family." Eloise asked Paula, "Why do you say that?" Paula said, "Girl, you got some long legs like they do!" Adreena quickly put her hand over Paula's mouth. Mrs. Zipperman didn't hear what Paula had said because she was talking with Mr. Jones. But Mrs. Jones heard her, and she gave Paula a strange look. Adreena looked at Paula with a smile on her face and said, "That was not nice to say." Paula said, "Well, Adreena, she does." Adreena said, "Paula, hush!"

Eloise returned from the bathroom and sat back down at the table and continued to eat. Adreena started asking Eloise questions about softball. Adreena wanted to know if she had played any softball before. Eloise said that she hadn't played any softball before, but her mother had. Eloise said, "My mother played softball back in 1952 for a team in the city where she grew up." Adreena wanted to ask her one more question. "What was your mother's name?" Eloise said, "Her name is Margret Filmner." After hearing that, Adreena fell out of her chair, almost hitting her head on the floor. Paula helped Adreena up from the floor, and she asked her, "Are you okay?" And with a stunned look on her face, Adreena said, "Yeah, yeah, girl." Adreena couldn't believe what Eloise had just said.

Eloise then told Adreena and Paula that when she was in school she had tried out for the football team. The coach had wanted her to play wide receiver because she was so tall, but she did not want to. Paula asked why. Eloise said, "The quarterback could not throw the ball high enough for me to catch it." Paula said, "What?" Eloise laughed and said, "Just kidding." Then Eloise said, "The men's basketball coach also wanted me to try out for the basketball team, so I did and I made it—but I quit."

Paula asked, "Why?" Eloise said, "Well, back in the day when I played, you were not allowed to slam or dunk the ball. But since I was so tall, it was easy for me to reach the rim and just put the ball in. But

A PITCHER TO REMEMBER

some of the boys couldn't, and I would always knock them down, and they would get mad and want to fight me." Paula mumbled to herself, "I can believe that."

Adreena punched Paula in the arm. As Adreena and Paula were talking with Eloise, there was another knock at the door. It was Paula's mother. Mrs. Jones asked Mrs. Jackson to come in, and she asked her, "How was the dinner party?" Mrs. Jackson said it was okay. Then Paula and her mother got ready to leave. And Paula told Adreena that she would see her later. Mrs. Zipperman and her granddaughter Eloise were leaving also. Mr. Jones said to everyone that he hoped they had enjoyed dinner. After everyone left Mrs. Jones said to Adreena, "I suggest that you go upstairs and get ready for bed, young lady. It's getting late."

After Adreena got out of the shower and put her pajamas on, she lay down in bed. But before she went to sleep, she picked up her favorite book and continued to read where she had left off:

After Turner went home, Viola went back downstairs and had dinner with her family. After dinner Viola went to her brother's room. She asked Demi, "Do you think it's possible that one day I could pitch for a professional baseball team?" Demi said, "Sis, you could pitch in any league you want to." That made Viola feel good about herself, and before she left Demi's room, she gave him a big hug. Viola then went to bed with a big smile on her face.

Viola's mother came into her room to check on her and gave her a big kiss on the cheek. "Goodnight, Viola." The next morning came around; and it was Saturday, so Viola didn't have to worry about going to school. She had been awakened by the smell of fresh bacon and eggs. Viola got up and got dressed.

When Viola came into the kitchen, everyone was sitting at the table, and Viola's mother asked her, "What do you have planned for the day?" She told her mother that the team from school was going to watch the Junction Clowns play for the championship game that day, so she was going with them. Viola said that the Junction Clowns would be playing a team from Florida called the Florida Rockets. Demi and her mom both said that they would like to come along, but they would leave after they finished eating breakfast.

Viola quickly finished up her breakfast, because she knew her teammates were waiting for her at the corner down by Craters Grocery Store. As Viola was leaving her house, she heard someone calling her name, "Viola! Viola!" She smiled and said to herself, "Turner. I would recognize that voice anywhere." And sure enough, when Viola turned around, she saw that it was Turner. He asked Viola, "Where are you going?" Viola told Turner that she and the rest of the team were going over to Murphy's Field to watch the Junction Clowns play because today was the big championship game.

Turner asked Viola if he could come along, and she said, "Let me ask the rest of the team." Viola's teammates were standing on the corner when she showed up with Turner. Lucy asked Viola, "What is Turner doing here?" Viola told Lucy that he wanted to come along. Lucy and the rest of the team said they didn't have a problem with that. So Turner, Viola, and her teammates finally made it over to Murphy's Field.

When they arrived, they saw the Junction Clowns warming up. Viola saw Coach Roy talking with one of his players, Mary Johnson, whom everyone called Peanut. Coach Roy came over to the fence where Viola and her teammates were standing. Coach Roy asked them, "How are you doing?" They answered, "We're doing okay." Coach Roy asked Viola, "Who is the little guy you have with you?" Viola said, "He's my friend Turner, and he lives down the street from me. And he wants to play professional baseball one day."

Coach Roy told Turner, "Just keep on trying and working hard at it, and you will get there." The umpire yelled out to both coaches, "Play ball!" Viola, Turner, and her teammates all went to sit in the stands so they could watch the game. Wilma Jackson, the catcher on Viola's team, asked Viola, "Who are the Junction Clowns playing?" Viola said, "They are playing a team from Florida called the Florida Rockets."

Viola told her teammates that the Florida Rockets had a good record. Viola's teammate Mattie Brown, who played right field, said, "The Rockets are an undefeated team." Viola said to herself, "I hope the Clowns can beat them." The pitcher for the Junction Clowns was Peanut, and the catcher was Wanda Jane, or "Scoops." They called her that because she scooped up anything and everything that the batters missed.

Again the umpire yelled, "Play ball!" The first batter up to hit from the Florida Rockets was Nettie Bates. Peanut threw her first pitch, and Nettie hit the ball. She started running toward first base, but the ball went foul, and the umpire yelled, "Foul ball!" Peanut threw her second pitch, and Nettie tried to hit the ball, but she missed. The umpire yelled, "Strike one!"

Nettie grabbed her towel from her back pocket to wipe the sweat off her face. She looked at Peanut, and Peanut smiled. Then Peanut looked over at Coach Roy, and he shook his head from side to side. He knew Peanut had something up her sleeve. Peanut picked up some red clay from the pitchers mound and rubbed it around the ball. Peanut then threw her third ball. Nettie swung and missed. "Strike three!" Viola jumped up from her seat and yelled out, "Good job, Peanut!" Nettie dropped her head and went back to the dugout.

Coach Roy yelled out to Peanut, "Good job!" The umpire yelled out, "Batter up!" The second batter up was Justine Pykes. Justine was known for the infield pop-and-fly, so Peanut knew she had to watch out for the ball. Peanut threw her first pitch to Justine; she hit the ball, and it went straight to Tonya Stone who played at second base. Tonya caught it, and Justine was out. Turner, Viola, and her teammates all jumped up and down and yelled, "Way to go, Junction Clowns!"

The third player up to bat for the Florida Rockets was Wahneta Strongs, their relief pitcher. Wahneta's specialty is hitting home runs. So Peanut didn't want to take any chances with her throws. When Wahneta stepped up to the batter's box Coach Roy asked the umpire to call time out. The umpire yelled, "Time!" Coach Roy walked out to the pitcher's mound where Peanut was standing, and he told her to not hold back on anything.

When Coach Roy said that, Peanut looked at him with a big smile. The umpire yelled, "Play ball!" Then Coach Roy hurried back to the Junction Clowns dugout. Peanut stared Wahneta straight in the face. Then Scoops, the catcher for the Junction Clowns, gave Peanut the signal on what kind of ball she should throw. Peanut nodded her head in agreement.

Peanut took a deep breath and threw the first pitch. Wahneta stepped up a little closer inside the batter's box; she swung and hit the ball. The crowd stood up and got very quiet.

The ball looked like it was going to go over the tall wooden fence. But out of nowhere, Junction Clowns center fielder Pearl Davis jumped up as high as she could and used part of the fence wall for leverage and came back down with the ball. Boy, the crowd went wild! The cheering was so loud you could've heard it in the next town.

Mary Hunt, center fielder on Viola's team, yelled out, "Pearl, I know how you feel, girl!" As the crowd continued to cheer, the Junction Clowns ran off the field and into the dugout, it was their turn to show the Florida Rockets what their team was made of.

Then the Florida Rockets ran out onto the field in their dark red and white uniforms. Their pitcher was Lula Roberts, and their catcher was Sarah Bennett, who was ranked second best in the league. Peanut was the first player up to hit for the Junction Clowns. Peanut stepped up to the plate, and Lula threw her first pitch. Peanut hit the ball, and Lula turned around fast to see where the ball was going. The ball went over the wall.

The crowd went wild, and everyone cheered and yelled as loud as they could. Viola and her teammates cheered for Peanut. The Junction Clowns had scored one run over the Rockets. The game went on for several innings, and the score was still one to zero; the Clowns were ahead.

It was the bottom of the ninth inning, and it had been a tough game throughout for both teams. The Junction Clowns were back on the field, and Peanut wasn't doing very well. She was starting to show signs of stress, and Coach Roy was getting worried about her. The Rockets were continuing to hang in there; they have never been beaten before.

The umpire yelled out, "Batter up!" The Rockets were continuing on with their batting order. The next person to hit was Penny Thomas; she was known for hitting line drives. Mable Green, who played shortstop on Viola's team, asked Viola, "Do you know who that is getting ready to hit?" Viola said, "Yes, I do, and Peanut had better watch out." Peanut threw the first pitch to Penny; she swung and missed.

The umpire yelled, "Strike one!" Peanut threw the second pitch, and Penny hit a line drive to Peanut. Penny ran for first base and made it. Peanut couldn't get out of the way of the ball quickly enough. The ball hit Peanut on her right thigh, and she went down. The crowd gasped and got really quiet. Turner, Viola, and her teammates all stood up in the stands, waiting intensely to see if Peanut was okay. You could have heard someone opening up a bottle of pop—it was just that quiet.

Coach Roy ran out onto the field. Peanut was in tears and holding on to her right thigh. Coach Roy was very concerned about Peanut. And, not having a relief pitcher to take her place, he didn't know what he was going to do. He started scratching his head. The umpire called time out, and he asked Coach Roy, "Do you have a relief pitcher?"

Coach Roy told the umpire that his relief pitcher hadn't shown up that day. Coach Roy had to figure out what he was going to do. So he called his team in off the field to talk to them. He told them, "Peanut got hit pretty hard in her thigh, and she's hurting really bad. So we need another pitcher because Emma Joe didn't show up." Then Tonya, who played second base, came up with a good idea. She said coach, "Why don't we ask Viola?" Coach Roy said, "That sounds like a great idea, but I have to follow the rules."

The umpire walked up to Coach Roy and asked him, "What are you going to do?" Coach Roy said to the umpire, "Well, if it's okay with Coach Lando, I would like to bring in a player I've been working with. But she is up in the stands." So the umpire walked over to Coach Lando Barnes of the Florida Rockets. And the umpire told Coach Lando that the Junction Clowns pitcher was hurt really badly and that they didn't have another pitcher. "So, Coach Roy wants to bring someone else in to pitch that he has been working with, if it's ok with you."

Coach Lando told the umpire that he thought it was against the rules. The umpire replied, "Not if you both agree on it." And then Coach Lando rationalized the situation and said out loud to himself, "We have never lost a game, and I don't want to forfeit this game—my team has worked hard to get here." Then Coach Lando said to the umpire, "Okay. Tell Coach Roy it's alright with me. They're going to lose anyway; they will never win this game. So, go ahead … Let them bring in that player they have been working with."

The umpire then walked back over to Coach Roy and told him that Coach Lando had said it would be okay with him. The umpire also mentioned to Coach Roy that Coach Lando had said the Clowns would never win the game. Coach Roy just laughed and then let his team know that he was going to ask Viola to pitch.

Coach Roy walked over to the stands where Viola and her teammates were sitting. Viola said, "Coach Roy, we saw Peanut get hit, and it looked pretty bad." Coach Roy said, "Yes, it is—and that's why I'm here. We need your help." Viola said, "Coach, what do you mean, you need my help?" Coach Roy told Viola that Peanut couldn't pitch anymore. "And my relief pitcher didn't show up. So, Viola I'm asking you, will you step in and pitch for me? The team and I need your help." Viola's eyes got big and she said, "You want me to do what?"

Coach Roy said, "I need you to pitch this last inning for me." Viola's teammates looked at her with big smiles on their faces. Then Susie, Wilma, Hattie, Lucy, Mable, Louise, Mattie, Mary, Amy, Margie, and

Thelma all cheered Viola on. Even little Turner cheered and gave Viola a big hug.

Viola told Coach Roy that she had never played professional baseball before. Coach Roy said, "Yes, Viola I know, but I believe you can do this. Please ... The team needs your help." Viola said, "Okay." Coach Roy then said to Viola, "Thank you." Viola walked into the locker room and went over to the bench where Peanut was sitting. Peanut said to Viola, "Do what you do best."

Viola gave Peanut a big smile, and she said, "Peanut, you do not have to worry. I will do my best for the team." Peanut gave Viola her uniform, and then Viola really felt like she was ready for the big leagues. She grabbed Peanut's mitt and ran out onto the field and to the pitcher's mound. The crowd started clapping and cheering her on.

You could hear Turner yelling out, "Viola! Viola!" But, little did she know, she had her work cut out for her. The umpire told Coach Roy, "Your pitcher has a few minutes to warm up." Viola threw a few pitches to the Junction Clowns catcher. Scoops yelled to Viola, "Good pitch!" Then the umpire called out, "Play ball!"

The Rockets second player up to bat was Blondie Gray; her specialty was baseline hitting, and she was the best in the league for splitting bases. You couldn't tell which way she was going to hit the ball. Viola didn't know anything about her, so all she could do was just pitch her best.

Viola threw her first pitch, and Blondie could see that it was coming fast. She pulled her bat back and tried to hit it as hard as she could, but she missed. The umpire yelled, "Strike one!" Then Viola got ready for her second pitch. Coach Roy had his hand over his face; he was nervous about what could happen next. Viola looked over at Coach Roy with a lot of confidence.

Viola threw her second pitch, and Blondie's eyes got big as two quarters. The ball was coming fast, but Blondie hit it and it went down the baseline toward third base. Penny ran to second base and made it, and Blondie made it to first. Coach Roy sat down in disbelief, scratched his head, and wiped the sweat from his forehead.

The next batter that walked up to the batter's box was Luz Jenkins. Luz was known for being the best in the league for bunting. She'd had a few offers from some other teams, but she only wanted to play ball for the Florida Rockets.

Viola threw her first pitch, and Luz missed it. Then Coach Roy called time out. He asked Viola, "Are you okay?" And with a big smile on her face, Viola told Coach Roy not to worry. With a worried look on his face, Coach Roy said, "Viola, don't forget this is for the championship." Viola said, "Yes, Coach, I know." Viola kept herself together. She remembered everything her brother Demi had taught her; he had never failed her yet. She remembered that she had been in situations like this before, even though this was her first time playing against a professional baseball team. The umpire yelled, "Play ball!" Coach Roy ran back to the dugout, where the rest of the team was. Viola threw her second pitch, and Luz hit the ball foul. The umpire yelled, "Foul!" Coach Lando of the Rockets yelled out to Luz, "Straighten it out!"

The crowd at Murphy's Field became very quiet for a few minutes. Viola scraped her shoes across the top of the plate on the pitcher's mound. Then she threw her third pitch to Luz, and Luz got the bunt like she always did in other games. As Viola was running for the bunt, she slipped, and so did Wanda Jane. Luz made it to first base. Blondie was now on second base, and Penny was on third base. The bases were loaded. Coach Roy called time out again. Viola walked over to the dugout, and Peanut came limping out. She said to Viola, "You have one more batter to pitch to. You can do this—just stay focused and believe in yourself." The umpire yelled, "Batter up!"

The next batter to come walking out of the dugout was Margret Filmner, the Florida Rockets surprised player. Viola turned around and looked; she couldn't believe who was getting ready to hit. Lucy and the rest of Viola's teammates couldn't believe that Margret Filmner was

A PITCHER TO REMEMBER

playing for the Florida Rockets. Lucy then said, "That's okay. Viola has got this wrapped up." Viola threw her first pitch really fast. She wanted to let Margret know that it wasn't going to be easy. Margret swung and missed the ball. The umpire yelled, "Strike one!"

The Junction Clowns crowd jumped up and started cheering and yelling for Viola. Margret looked back at them like she didn't like what she was hearing. Just before Viola started to throw her second pitch, she heard someone yelling, "You're doing a great job, honey!" Viola looked in the direction of the voice. It was Viola's mother and her brother Demi. She gave them a big smile. Then Viola threw her second pitch. The umpire yelled, "Ball!" Wanda Jane threw the ball back to Viola.

Viola got ready to throw the ball again and then turned to the field to look for any runners. She saw Blondie headed for third base; Luz was headed to second. Their teammate Penny was yelling to them, "Go back! Go back!" Viola quickly threw the ball to Tonya Stone on second base, and she got Blondie out. Then Cynthia Morgan ran up from shortstop; Tonya threw her the ball, and she got Luz out.

The crowd went crazy. Penny just stood on third base with a stunned look on her face. Viola was shocked; she could not believe that she had just helped the Junction Clowns get out some of the Florida Rockets players. Viola then realized that was only two outs, and Margaret Filmner was still standing in the batter's box. Viola could see that Margaret was very upset about her teammates getting out. So Viola composed herself for the pitch. The score was still Junction Clowns one and the Florida Rockets zero.

Viola was getting ready to throw the ball to Margret when remembered the last time she had pitched to Margret, back in middle school. Viola had thrown the famous ball that her brother had taught her. She dug her shoes into the red clay, so she wouldn't fall. Margret started sweating like someone was pouring water on her; she was just that upset.

The ball came across the plate, and Margret tried to hit it; but the ball hit Scoops's glove so hard you could see the dust come off it. Scoops took her hand out of the glove really fast and shook it. The umpire yelled, "Strike three! You're out!" Margaret looked at Viola and then at the umpire and then walked off to the dugout. Viola couldn't believe what had just happened. The Junction Clowns had won the game. The crowd in the stands jumped up and started yelling really loudly. You would think it was the Fourth of July. Viola's teammates, her mother, brother, dad, and Turner were very excited and glad to see that Viola had pulled the game off.

That was the first championship game that the Junction Clowns had ever won. The entire team ran out onto the field to congratulate Viola on what a great job of pitching she had done. Coach Roy was excited and happy that his team was the team the Florida Rockets had their first loss of the season—and the championship game—to.

Coach Lando Barnes and the rest of the Florida Rockets walked over to congratulate the Junction Clowns on what a great game they had played. Coach Lando told Coach Roy that Viola was quite a pitcher. And Coach Roy said, "Yes, I know."

As the Junction Clowns were loading up on the bus for a long ride home, Viola ran up to Coach Roy and asked him if she could keep the uniform. Coach Roy said, "Yes, keep it—it's yours. You've worked really hard for it." Peanut gave Viola a big hug and told her that she had done an awesome job out there that day. Viola said, "Thanks, Peanut. That means a lot coming from you." Viola then told Coach Roy that playing for the Junction Clowns had been the chance of a lifetime. "Thanks for giving that to me," she said. As the bus drove away from Murphy's Field, Coach Roy looked back at Viola as she stood there watching them leave and told his team that Viola was definitely a pitcher to remember.

Viola became well known in high school as one of the most versatile players in softball to use her pitching skills in fast pitch and playing in a professional baseball game with the Junction Clowns. A few years passed, and Viola and her Burnsfield Cats teammates all graduated from high school and went off to college. No one heard from Viola after that. Some of the players became teachers, doctors, and also softball coaches. It was said that Viola could be coaching a professional team up north somewhere. Turner became a professional pitcher with the L.A. Dodgers. And every time he'd pitch the ball he would have a big smile on his face. Turner just knew that Viola was somewhere watching her little friend from down the street. Demi Smith became a professional baseball coach for the Philadelphia Phillies.

Adreena finished reading the last pages of her book and then she went to sleep.

The years passed, and soon enough it was 1983. Adreena is in her last year of high school. The past two years of high school has been tough for the team. They had always made the playoffs but had never won a championship. The Montville Wild Tigers had one more game to play for the season, and if they won they would be state champions.

One Friday, Coach Lawson made an announcement over the intercom system saying that there would be softball practice that day. He also reminded everyone the championship game would be played there at the school on the following day. "So, come and show your support for the team." Coach Lawson and Coach Connie met with the girls in the gymnasium. Coach Connie called out the girls' names one by one: Adreena, Paula, Candy, Keisha, Jennifer, Shala, Leslie, Sheila, Ashley, Judy, Pamela, Amy, Porsha, and Janie.

After roll call, Coach Connie started to talk with the team. She said, "It's been a long three years, and we have finally made it to a championship game. Tomorrow we'll be put to the test. We will be playing against the best team in our division, the Jacksonville Cats from Florida, and they have not lost a game this season. But they will be playing against us, and we must hand them their first loss."

When Coach Connie said that, the team started clapping and getting really fired up about the game. Coach Connie said, "I just want to let each and every one of you know that you are so special. And you girls have a special bond. As long as I have been coaching, this is the first time that I've seen a team get along like you do." When Coach Connie said that, you could see the big smiles on their faces.

Coach Connie started crying, and the girls got up from where they were sitting and gathered around her. They gave her a big group hug. Then Paula said, "Hey! I thought this was supposed to be practice." And with a grin on her face Adreena looked at Paula and said, "Girl, you just don't know when to stop."

The girls turned and looked at Coach Lawson and said to him, "Coach, do you have anything else you need to say to us?" Coach Lawson said, "Well yes I do." He said, "Girls, this is one of the best teams I have ever coached, and I am so proud of each and every one of you. Let's be ready to play tomorrow. I want every one of you to go home and get a good night's sleep, and I will see you here tomorrow. The game starts at six thirty in the evening, but I want you to be here at five."

As the girls were leaving, Coach Lawson and Coach Connie called Adreena and Paula over and asked them to wait because they wanted to talk to them. Coach Lawson told them that he was going to start Paula first tomorrow because Adreena was pretty good at closing the game out.

Both Adreena and Paula thought that was a good idea. The girls felt like Coach Lawson and Coach Connie knew what they were doing. Adreena and Paula left the gym after talking with both of the coaches. While they were walking back toward the locker room to pick up their books to go home, Paula got ready to tell Adreena a joke.

Paula said, "Adreena, what's yellow and has a lot of appeal?" Adreena said, "I don't know, Paula. Girl, what are you talking about?" Paula said, "Adreena, just answer the question." Adreena said, "Okay, Paula, I give up. What is it?" Paula says, "A banana." Adreena laughs and looks at Paula. "Girl, you have lost your mind." Both of them start laughing and tell each other, "See you tomorrow." Saturday evening came around quickly, and one by one, the members of the Montville Wild Tigers team started showing up in the school's locker room. You could tell that they are really happy about playing in the championship game. Everyone was laughing, and they had music playing—you would have thought that they were at a party.

Adreena came walking through the door, and she had the biggest smile on her face. She sat in front of her locker and took out her old blue and white number 7 jersey. She wanted to look at it for one last time before her last game. Keisha walked over to where Adreena was sitting, and she asked Adreena, "Are you okay?" Adreena said, "Yeah, I am doing okay. It is just that I cannot believe that this is our last year in high school—and we finally get to play in our first championship game for our team."

Coach Connie and Coach Lawson walked into the locker room for the last time as the coaches of this team. Coach Lawson told the team, "Coach Connie and I need you to remember and know that we have enjoyed coaching each and every one of you and having you on our team. So, go out there and give it your all and play your best. And remember not to take the Jacksonville Cats team lightly. They haven't lost a game all season, so be prepared to work hard for this championship title."

Coach Connie asked them all to bow their heads to pray. After the team finished saying their special prayer, they started walking outside. The home crowd started cheering the Montville Wild Tigers on. The whole team had big grins on their faces. Adreena heard someone yelling her name, "Adreena! Adreena!" It was her mom and dad. Adreena waved and smiled at them. The Montville Wild Tigers ran out onto the field to warm up.

Keisha Brown (#6) was playing third base. Paula Jackson (#2) was on the pitcher's mound; Jennifer Williams (#9) was playing first base. Shala Davis (#8) was on second base; Leslie Johnson (#17) was out in right field. Sheila Hill (#40) was in center field; Ashley Willis (#45) had left field covered. Amy Banks (#55) was playing shortstop; Judy Palkins (#19) was also playing shortstop. Jany Palmer (#11) was relief pitcher; Pamela Jameson (#15), who was known as P.J., and Porsha Hamilton (#2) were the designated hitters. In addition, there were Adreena Jones (#7), pitcher, and Candy Walker (#18), catcher.

The Montiville Wild Tigers team started to warm up, and everyone was looking their best. The old blue and white really looked good under the lights at night. While their team was out on the field warming up, Coach Lawson and Coach Connie talked about what might happen during the game.

And as they talked, the crowd got louder. The Jacksonville Cats were getting ready to take the field and warm up. Coach Lawson called his team off the field. He asked everyone to take a seat in the dugout and rest up a little bit while the Cats warmed up.

Coach Lawson asked Sheila and some of his other big hitters to pay close attention to the Jacksonville Cats pitcher. He said the young lady wearing #12 was Kim Peeler "And she has a mean curve ball," he added. Then Coach Lawson said, "She is the best in the league." Coach Lawson wanted to make sure his team watched Kim Peeler's pitch very closely when they got up to hit.

While the Montiville Wild Tigers were watching the Jacksonville Cats warm up, they noticed how every ball was thrown and every ball was caught. Jennifer said, "Boy! They really look good." Adreena paid close attention to the Jacksonville Cats pitcher. Adreena noticed how every time Kim Peeler released the ball there was a mean look on her face. Paula walked up to Adreena in the dugout and told her, "You don't have to worry—don't let her scare you."

The umpire signaled over to the Jacksonville Cats coaches, Felicia McCarthy and Mike Peeks, and told them that it was time to get their players off the field so they could start the game. You could hear the crowd cheering their favorite teams on while the umpire went over the

A PITCHER TO REMEMBER

rules with the coaches from both teams. After the umpire finished talking with the coaches, he yelled, "Batter up!"

The first team up to hit was the Montiville Wild Tigers; it would only seem right since they had home field advantage. The first player to hit was Paula Jackson (#2). And Kim Peeler (#12), the Jacksonville Cats pitcher, was warming up and throwing fast. The Jacksonville Cats catcher, Hazel Smokes (#10), was catching them without any problem.

Again the umpire yelled, "Batter up!" Paula had this worried look on her face. Adreena yelled out to Paula from the dugout, "Remember what you told me!" Paula shakes her head from side to side and said to herself, "Adreena, you just don't know." Kim threw her first pitch. Paula swung and missed.

The umpire yelled, "Strike one!" Coach Lawson yelled out from the dugout, "Take your time, Paula!" The home crowd was cheering for Paula. Hazel threw the ball back to Kim, who picked up some red clay and rubbed it on the ball. The Jacksonville Cats coach, Mike Peeks, yelled out to her, "Make this one count!"

Kim threw her second ball, and Paula got a really tight grip on the bat. She could feel that this one was going to have some smoke behind it. Paula swung and hit the ball; the home crowd jumped up from their seats. The ball went between the first baseman Rachel Waters (#13) and shortstop Alie Green (#4). And Paula ran as fast as she could toward first base.

The Cats left fielder Jessica Thompson (#28) threw the ball back to their pitcher, Kim. Paula's teammates were jumping up and down in the dugout; they were happy because Paula made it to first base. Kim, the Cats pitcher, shook her head with disbelief as she looked at her first baseman and shortstop Alie. She said, "Come on, guys. Let's get it together." The second player up to hit was the Tigers third baseman Keisha Brown (#6). She had walked up to the batter's box with all the confidence in the world. You could tell she was ready to play by the way she was swinging her bat.

The Cats pitcher Kim was warming up for the next batter. The umpire yelled, "Batter up!" Kim took a deep breath and looked to the dugout at Coach Felicia and then back to the Cats catcher, Hazel. Keisha was staring at Kim with a serious look on her face. Kim threw her first pitch, and it was coming straight at Keisha. She took a swing at the ball and misses it. The umpire yelled, "Strike one!" The ball hit Hazel's glove like someone had shot a cannon off.

The Cats crowd started clapping and then someone from the Tigers crowd yelled out, "You'll get the next one, Keisha!" You could see the smile on Keisha's face when she heard that comment. Hazel threw the ball back to Kim. And Kim wiped the sweat off her head. She felt and knew how tense this tournament was because she had been here before.

Kim got ready to throw her second pitch; she wound up and then released the ball. You could almost see the wind behind it. Keisha swung at the ball, and again she missed it. "Strike two!" Keisha stepped back from the batter's box; she picked up some red clay and rubbed it on the bat for good luck. But before Keisha could step back into the batter's box, Coach Connie called time out and ran over to Keisha and whispered something into her ear. Keisha nodded her head in agreement.

The umpire yelled, "Batter up!" Kim threw her third pitch; Keisha hit a pop fly ball, and Kathy Cealer (#20), the center fielder for the Cats, got under the ball and yelled out, "I got it!" Paula took off for second base; Kathy Cealer caught the pop fly, so Paula had to hurry up and get back to first base. She made it.

The Jacksonville Cats had just given the Montville Wild Tigers their first out. And the fans from Jacksonville were cheering really loud for their Cats, letting them know how happy they were about what had just happened. The next player up to hit was Candy Walker (#18), the Tigers catcher. Candy tightened her gloves; she wanted to make sure she hit the ball hard because the Tigers needed to get on the scoreboard. Candy knew the Cats were a tough team, but she was determined to hit the ball. Kim Peeler was getting ready to throw her first ball to Candy.

Kim wound up and released the ball. Candy saw it coming fast and hard. Candy swung and hit the ball straight to center field where Kathy Cealer was positioned. Kathy backed up to the wall, and she jumped up and tried to catch the ball—but the ball went over the wall! Paula rounded the bases and made it into home. Candy Walker crossed home plate right behind her. Then Candy looked at Hazel and smirked. "Nice uniform," she added. Candy had hit the first home run of the night for the Montville Wild Tigers.

Coach Lawson, Coach Connie, and the rest of the team ran from the dugout to meet Candy after she crossed home plate. The Tigers fans went wild; they could not believe that the Montville Wild Tigers had just scored two runs on the undefeated Jacksonville Cats. Now the score was two to zero, and the Cats had one out against the Tigers. Coach Lawson told the team, "We have to keep it together and stay focused."

The next batter up to hit for the Tigers was first baseman Jennifer Williams (#9). She stood six foot one and had a mean swing. After Kim Peeler finished warming up, the umpire yelled, "Batter up!"

Jennifer walked up to the batter's box, and the Jacksonville fans started booing her. Coach Connie yelled out to Jennifer, "Don't worry about that—just focus on the game!" So Jennifer shook off the distraction of the booing. Kim threw her first ball, and Jennifer stepped back from it. The umpire yelled, "Strike one!" Hazel threw the ball back to Kim. Then Kim turned around and gave her shortstop Alie the thumbs up, letting her know that it was okay—she had it under control.

And then Kim leaned down and picked up some red clay and rubbed it all over the ball so she could grip it more tightly. Kim started to chew her gum really quickly as she threw her second ball to Jennifer. It looked like it was going to the outside, so Jennifer reached over with those long arms of hers and hit a pop fly out into right field. Mattie Williams (#23), the right fielder for the Cats, got under it and made the catch. The Montville Wild Tigers fans started to boo really loudly; they didn't like that play. The Jacksonville Cats just needed one more out before they could show the Tigers why they were the best team in the league. Jennifer walked back to the dugout with her head down; she was feeling bad about the play that had just happened. Coach Connie gave Jennifer a big hug and then looked her straight in the eye and said, "Don't you feel bad; you will do better next time."

Next up to hit was Shala Davis (#8), the Tigers second baseman. This was her first year playing softball, and the funny thing about Shala was that she liked to smile a lot, no matter what the situation was. The umpire yelled, "Batter up!" Shala walked up to the batter's box. The Cats catcher, Hazel, asked her, "What are you smiling about?" Shala didn't answer her; she just kept on smiling. Hazel shook her head and said to herself, "I guess you never know what kind of people you will meet." Hazel showed no fear and tried not to let Shala's smiling faze her at all because she knew what needed to be done to make the game turn out the way she wanted it to. The umpire yelled, "Play ball!" And just as Shala was getting into position to hit the ball, Kim stopped and looked down at the pitcher's plate. Then she reached down to clean it off.

The umpire called time, and Hazel walked out to the pitcher's mound to talk with Kim. She said to her, "I don't know why this girl is smiling so much." Kim told Hazel, "Don't worry. I'm going to wipe that smile right off her face." Kim finished cleaning off the pitcher's plate, and the umpire yelled, "Play ball!" Hazel ran back to the catcher's position. Kim gave Shala a serious look, but it didn't faze her at all—she just kept smiling. Kim threw her first pitch to Shala; Shala swung hard, but she missed it. The umpire yelled, "Strike one!" Hazel threw the ball back to Kim. Shala looked back at Hazel, still smiling, and Hazel gave Shala a strange look and said to herself, "I wonder if this girl is on any medication."

Before Kim threw the second ball to Shala, she looked over at her coaches in the dugout. Coach McCarthy shrugged her shoulders as if to say to Kim that she didn't know why Shala was smiling so much either. Shala had everyone puzzled about why she was constantly smiling. Then

A PITCHER TO REMEMBER

Kim looked back at Shala and threw her second ball. You could almost see the wind follow the ball as it reached Shala. She swung, and again she missed. The umpire yelled, "Strike two!" The ball hit Hazel's glove so hard it made a really loud noise.

The fans of the Montville Wild Tigers were very confused about Shala. She had just got a second strike on her, yet she was still smiling. She was smiling so wide you could count her teeth. Hazel said to Shala, "Do you need your brain checked or what?" But that didn't faze Shala at all either; she just continued to smile. Coach Lawson was wondering whether he should call a time out or not. So Coach Lawson yelled out to Shala, "Are you okay?" And Shala turned around with that big smile still planted on her face and nodded her head yes that she was okay. Kim signaled to the infield to move in just a little. The umpire yelled, "Play ball!" Kim stepped back and leaned forward, throwing the ball the hardest she had thrown it yet that night.

The ball was coming very fast, and you could see Shala blinking her eyes but still smiling. Shala bunted the ball and took off running as fast as she could to first base. Kim and Hazel ran after the ball; and while they are doing that, Shala had made it past first base and was rounding to second. She left second and was making her way to third when Kim threw to Tiffie White (#5), the Cats third baseman—who missed the ball. Shala was making her way into home as Tiffie picked up the ball and threw it in to Hazel. Shala slid into home plate and Hazel met her there. As the umpire was making the call, the fans from both the Jacksonville Cats and the Montville Wild Tigers got really quiet. Then the umpire yelled, "Safe!" Shala got up and brushed herself off, looked back at Hazel and Kim, smiled, and started walking toward the dugout.

The Tigers came running out of the dugout and cheered for Shala. The home team fans were yelling, "Shala! Shala!" And as Kim and Hazel of the Jacksonville Cats started to walk back to their playing positions they stopped and said to each other, "Now we know why she was smiling so much—the girl is good!" The score was now Montville

Wild Tigers, three, and the Jacksonville Cats, zero. The next batter up to hit for the Tigers was right fielder Leslie Johnson (#17). Leslie was known for her seriousness; she didn't like to play around too much.

The umpire yelled, "Batter up!" Leslie stepped up to the plate and dug in. The Cats pitcher Kim has a discouraged look on her face, but she was determined to keep her pitching sharp. Hazel gave Kim different signals about which ball to throw to Leslie. Kim nodded her head in agreement with Hazel about one of the pitches that she had chosen. Then Kim pitched the ball; Leslie swung and missed. The umpire yelled, "Strike one!" Hazel threw the ball back to Kim, and then Kim looked around at the crowd. The Cats fans were yelling out to her, "Come on, girl! You can do it!" Kim stepped off the mound for a few seconds to think about what pitch to throw to Leslie next.

Then Kim walked back onto the mound, pulled her hair back from her face, and threw a hard pitch. Leslie was very nervous, she swung and hit the ball; but it went up into the air and behind her. Hazel was yelling, "I got it! I got it!" Kim ran up to catch the ball just in case Hazel missed it. But the ball fell right into Hazel's glove. The Cats finally got their third out.

All of the Jacksonville Cats fans jumped up from their seats and started cheering and clapping for their home team. Kim walked into the dugout and said to Coach McCarthy and Coach Peeks, "I didn't think we were ever going to get out of that." Coach McCarthy said "They are a tougher team to beat than we thought they would be."

It was now time for the Montville Wild Tigers to take the field, but before they did Coach Lawson told them that he was going to let Paula pitch first. Paula asked Coach Lawson, "Are you sure?" Coach Lawson said, "Yes, Paula, I am. I have confidence in you." The score: Tigers, three; Cats, zero.

The Montville Wild Tigers started to warm up, and Paula Jackson (#2) was on the pitcher's mound. The umpire yelled, "Play ball!" The first batter up to hit for the Jacksonville Cats was pitcher Kim Peeler

(#12). Paula kicked the red clay from around the plate on the pitcher's mound. She wanted to make sure that there wasn't anything to get in the way of doing what she did best. Then Paula looked over at Adreena in the dugout, and Adreena gave her the thumbs up sign to let her know that she would be okay.

Paula threw her first pitch to Kim. She was holding the bat up high over her right shoulder; then she dropped it fast to try to hit the ball, but she missed it. The ball hit the glove of Candy Walker (#18), the catcher for the Tigers. The umpire yelled, "Strike one!" Candy threw the ball back to Paula.

And then Paula reached down and picked up some red clay to rub on her hands so she could grip the ball better. Candy then signaled to Paula to throw a curve ball this time, and Paula nodded her head okay. Paula pulled her right sleeve up onto her shoulder so she could get an even better throw in this time. Paula threw her second ball to Kim, and it came straight down the middle. Again Kim held the bat up high over her right shoulder.

Kim hit the ball right out to center field where Sheila Hill (#40) was positioned. She saw the ball coming and made the adjustment to catch it, but it went over the wall. Kim had hit the first home run for the Jacksonville Cats, and the Jacksonville fans went crazy. When Kim crossed home plate, her teammates ran out of the dugout to meet her with hugs and cheers.

Coach McCarthy said, "Good job, Kim." The Cats let the Tigers know they were back in the game. The score was now Tigers, three, and Cats, one. The second batter up to hit for the Cats was their catcher, Hazel Smokes (#10). Hazel always sang in a low tone to herself when she was up to bat. It helped her with calming her nerves.

The umpire yelled, "Play ball!" Hazel continued to sing to herself as she waited on Paula's pitch. Candy, the Tigers catcher, asked Hazel, "What is it you're singing?" And Hazel said, "It's just a song about a clown." Candy thought to herself, *This girl is kind of odd.* Paula threw her first pitch to Hazel, and as the ball got closer to Hazel, she started to sing louder and louder. And she swung and missed the ball. The umpire yelled, "Strike one!" Hazel dropped her head in shame.

The hometown fans for the Tiger were dancing in the stands. Hazel didn't know what to think. She was puzzled, but she knew that she had to keep her head in the game. Paula didn't want to waste any time getting ready to throw her second pitch. Candy threw the ball back to Paula, and then Paula noticed that her shoelace was untied. She reached down and tied it very tight. She had to make sure she kept things going.

The wind was starting to blow just a little, but that wouldn't stop Paula from doing the job she had to do to try to win the ball game. Paula threw the second pitch to Hazel, and she was so nervous that her right leg started to shake uncontrollably. She swung and missed again. The umpire yelled out, "Strike two!" Hazel looked over at the Cats dugout; Coach McCarthy could see that something was wrong, so she called a time out. She asked Hazel, "Why are you shaking so much? Are you okay?" Hazel nervously said, "Yes, I'm okay. I just need to get a hold of myself and calm my nerves down."

After Coach McCarthy finished talking with Hazel she walked back to the dugout. Coach Peeks asked Coach McCarthy, "Is Hazel okay?" Coach McCarthy said, "Yes, she is just really nervous, but she will be okay." Hazel took her batting helmet off and wiped the tears from her eyes. She was starting to feel the pressure. The umpire yelled, "Play ball!" Paula took a deep breath. Candy gave Paula the signal on what pitch to throw next, and Paula nodded okay and threw the ball. Hazel wasn't sure of herself; but she swung and hit the ball. It was a line drive straight into Paula's right arm. Hazel took off running to first base, and she made it. Paula grabbed her arm and fell to the ground.

Everyone in the stands got quiet. Coach Lawson and Coach Connie ran out onto the field to see how badly Paula was hurt. The umpire yelled, "Time!" Coach Lawson asked Paula was she okay. With tears in her eyes, she said, "Yes, Coach. I'm okay." Coach Connie said to Paula,

A PITCHER TO REMEMBER

"You got hit in your throwing arm." Then Coach Connie pulled back the sleeve to see how badly Paula had gotten hit. Coach Connie said, "Boy, you've got a red mark there. Coach Lawson thought it would be a good idea to call in another pitcher, but Paula said, "No, Coach, I'll be alright." Coach Lawson replied, "I have to do what I need to do right now. I may need you later on." Paula said, "Well, what about Adreena?" Coach Lawson said, "No, not now. I may need Adreena to close the game out."

After Coach Lawson and Coach Connie finished making sure that Paula was okay, they took her back to the dugout. The Tigers and Cats fans clapped and gave Paula a standing ovation for being able to take a hit like that and walk away from it. Coach Lawson decided to replace Paula with Jany Palmer (#11). Coach Lawson looked Jany straight in the eye and said, "Do the best that you can …. We can take this game." Jany ran out to the pitcher's mound and started warming up.

Then Coach Connie turned around, looked at Adreena, and said, "You will get your turn—just stay focused." Adreena said, "Don't worry, Coach Connie. I know it's just a matter of time. Jany finished warming up, the umpire yelled play ball!

The next up to bat for the Cats was third baseman Tiffie White (#5). Tiffie walked up to the batter's box, not sure what kind of pitches Jany would throw to her. She just knew that she had to be ready. Hazel was still on first base making sure she was paying close attention to their first base coach, Coach Peeks. Jany raised her arm and pitched her first ball to Tiffie. The ball was coming with a definite spin on it. Tiffie swung with all of her might, and she missed the ball. The umpire yelled, "Strike one!" Tiffie walked back and forth, hitting the bottom of her shoes with the bat to get the clay out of her cleats so she could stand better in the batters box. Before Jany threw her next pitch, Candy, the catcher for the Tigers, walked out to her and gave her a handshake for good luck.

Then Candy went back to her position behind home plate and started to give Jany different signals about what kind of ball to throw next. The Tigers had their own codes that they used to communicate with each other. Jany wound up and again pitched the ball to Tiffie. Tiffie stared at the ball as Jany released it; she swung and missed again. "Strike two!" The home team fans continued to show their love for the Montiville Wild Tigers.

The score was still Tigers, three, and Cats, one, with no outs. The Jacksonville Cats knew they needed something big to happen for them before this game got out of their hands. Candy, the Tigers catcher, threw the ball back to Jany. The umpire yelled, "Time!" Then he reached down to clean off home plate. Jany was standing on the pitcher's mound waiting on the umpire to let her know when she could throw the next ball.

The umpire yelled out, "Okay, play ball!" Jany turned and gave Hazel the look while she was on first base. She wanted to let Hazel know that she was going to have to move pretty fast to get to the second base without her knowing about it. Jany was setting her feet in place and visualizing her next pitch. Tiffie knew that this play would make or break her game, so she had to hit the ball. Jany pitched the ball like a rocket shooting into space. Tiffie hit it, and the ball went straight to right field, the same area where Leslie Johnson (#17) is positioned. Leslie set herself up to catch it, but it went over her head and over the wall.

Hazel rounded the bases, and Tiffie took off running and also rounded the bases. The Montiville Wild Tigers couldn't believe what had just happened. Hazel crossed home plate, and then along came Tiffie White. The Montiville Wild Tigers fans were in disbelief. They knew it was going to be tough for the Tigers to win after that. The Jacksonville Cats team came running out of the dugout to congratulate both Hazel and Tiffie on a job well done. The score was now Tigers, three, and Cats, three, making it a tied game with no outs. Coach Lawson said to Coach Connie, "And that is how the Cats got this far, playing just like that." The Montiville Wild Tigers continued to play hard, and finally they got three outs on the Jacksonville Cats.

Several innings passed, and the game was still tied three to three. It was the top of the ninth inning, and both teams had played great softball. Kim Peeler the Cats pitcher had been pitching a great game, but now she had to try to shut the Tigers down. The next batter up to hit for the Tigers was center fielder Sheila Hill (#40). Sheila had been known to steal bases, and she was pretty good at it. Kim knew she had her hands full with Sheila. Kim finished warming up, and the umpire yelled, "Batter up!" Kim knew that now she had to pitch the best she had ever pitched before. Kim threw her first pitch, and Sheila makes sure that she was inside the batter's box. Sheila swung and missed the ball. The umpire yelled, "Strike one!"

The Cats catcher Hazel said to Sheila, "Are you going to miss this one, too?" Then Sheila said to Hazel, "Just watch and see." Hazel threw the ball back to Kim, and you could see the tiredness on Kim's face. Her coach hadn't given her a break since the game started. Kim pitched the ball to Sheila for the second time, and it was coming so fast you could see the smoke from it. Sheila pulled back and swung. She hit the ball over to left field where the Jessica Thompson (#28) was positioned, and the ball dropped about five feet in front of her. Jessica picked it up as quickly as she could and threw it to first base to Rachael Waters (#13), but Sheila had already made it onto first base. Coach Lawson was there, and he told Sheila he needed her to play it safe when stealing bases.

Coach McCarthy of the Cats called a time out. She needed to talk with Kim to make sure she was alright. Coach McCarthy walked over to Kim and asked her if she was okay. Kim said, "Yes, just a little tired, but I can finish, Coach. Don't take me out of the game—let me finish it." Coach McCarthy said, "Okay, I'm going to keep my eyes on you to make sure you are alright. But as soon as I see that you're not, I'm going to take you out." Kim said, "Okay, Coach." So Coach McCarthy walked back to the dugout, and Coach Peeks asked her, "Is Kim okay?" Coach McCarthy said, "Yes, she will be alright."

The umpire yelled, "Play ball!" The next batter to hit for the Tigers was left fielder Ashley Willis (#45). Ashley was always one of those players who was good with statistics; she could tell you anything about the game you did not know. Ashley walked up to the batter's box, but before she got ready to hit she asked Hazel, "Can you tell me who was the best ever overall woman softball player?" Hazel gave Ashley a strange look; then she shrugged her shoulders and said no. Ashley then got ready to bat. Kim didn't waste any time. She quickly threw the ball, and Ashley swung the bat and hit a pop fly right to midfield. Kim yelled out, "I got it!" She caught the pop fly and then saw Sheila running toward second base.

Coach Lawson and the rest of the Tigers were yelling at Sheila, "Get back! Get back!" Sheila was running back as fast as she could, but Kim fired the ball off to Rachel at first base and got her out, making it a double play. Coach Lawson put his hands over his face in disbelief; he just could not believe the play that had just happened.

The Jacksonville Cats fans were jumping up and down, cheering and clapping and showing their support. They couldn't believe the double play the Jacksonville Cats had just made on the Montville Wild Tigers. Both Coach McCarthy and Coach Peeks were yelling out, "Boy, what a play! You girls are doing a great job!" And then Coach McCarthy yelled out to Kim, "One more time! One more time!"

The score was still tied: Tigers, three, and Cats, three, with two outs for the Tigers. The umpire yelled, "Play ball!" Next up to hit was the Tigers shortstop Amy Banks (#55). Amy had always been the one who was able to keep the team's spirits up. Before she walked up to the batter's box, she looked back at the dugout and told her teammates, "I'm going to hit one for the team."

It was now the bottom of the ninth inning. Amy was walking up to the batter's box; she knew that the team was depending on her to break the tie. Kim didn't know what to expect from Amy. But right then Kim had only one thing on her mind, and that was to win the game. Kim yelled to Hazel, "Are you ready?" Hazel yelled back, "Yeah!"

Amy was feeling the pressure, but she wasn't letting it show. She just got ready for the pitch. Kim stepped back—looked to her right and then to her left—and threw the ball. Amy quickly adjusted the way she was holding the bat, took a swing at the ball, and hit it straight down the center. Kim tried to jump up and catch it; but she couldn't reach it, and the ball went out to center field.

Amy had made her way to first base. Kathy Cealer (#20), the Cats center fielder, tried to get underneath the ball, but she missed it also. The ball dropped to the ground, and then rolled to the wall. Kathy ran after it, and in the meantime, Amy had already tagged second base and then third base. She headed toward home plate. Kathy finally reached the ball and threw it to Tiffie White (#5), the third baseman for the Cats. Tiffie caught the ball and then turned and looked toward home. Amy was headed straight for home plate. Tiffie yelled out, "Hazel!" That got her attention, and Tiffie threw the ball to Hazel.

Amy was caught between them, running back and forth. Hazel threw the ball back to Tiffie, and Tiffie threw the ball back to Hazel. The Tigers fans were yelling to Amy, "Go back! Go back! Go back!" And the Cats fans were yelling to Tiffie and Hazel, "Get her! Get her! Get her!" And the fans get louder and louder. All of the Coaches from both teams were yelling the same things from the dugout that their teams' fans were yelling.

Hazel threw the ball back to Tiffie—and Tiffie dropped it! Amy ran right past Hazel, crossing home plate. Hazel and her teammates just dropped their heads in disbelief. The Tigers had broken the tie: the score was now Tigers, four, and the Cats, three. The hometown fans of the Montville Wild Tigers were going crazy, clapping and cheering and yelling out, "Amy! Amy!" As Amy walked into the Tigers dugout, she yelled, "One for the home team!"

Coach Lawson and Coach Connie let the girls know that they were very proud of the whole team. "Keep up the good work, because the game isn't over with yet. We still have more batting to do." Coach Lawson sent out their designated hitter Pamela Jameson (#15), better known as P.J. She grabbed her favorite bat, the Louisville Slugger, as she walked out of the dugout to the batter's box. The Cats pitcher Kim was still warming up, so P.J. stood back and waited for Kim to finish.

Then Coach McCarthy walked out to the pitcher's mound where Kim was and told Kim, "You have done a great job this whole game, but I'm going to put in a relief pitcher now." Kim asked Coach McCarthy why, and her coach responded, "Kim, you have pitched the whole game up until now, and I can see that you're very tired. So I'm going to let you get some much deserved rest and put in our relief pitcher Leandra. She's going to pitch the rest of the game." Kim agreed with Coach McCarthy on switching out pitchers and said, "It's the best thing for the team."

Kim handed the ball over to Coach McCarthy, and the Jacksonville Cats fans started clapping and cheering and gave Kim a standing ovation. As Kim started to walk back toward the bench, Leandra Hart (#14) came out of the dugout saying, "Finish the game out where Kim left off." As they walked past each other, Kim slapped Leandra high five, and then Leandra headed toward the pitcher's mound.

Then Coach McCarthy stopped Leandra and told her, "Do your best to get this last out for us." Leandra threw a few pitches back and forth to Hazel to warm up. And every time Leandra threw the ball to Hazel, P.J. watched and studied her follow-through technique. The umpire asked Leandra if she was ready to play. Leandra answered yes. Then the umpire yelled, "Batter up!" P.J. stepped into the batter's box and then looked up into the stands, where her mother was sitting, and gave her a big smile. Leandra threw her first pitch, and P.J. swung and missed it. The umpire yelled, "Strike one!" Hazel threw the ball back to Leandra. And before Leandra threw out her second pitch to P.J., she stepped back from the pitcher's mound and took her glove off to tighten the strings on the thumb area. Leandra just wanted to make sure that nothing would be in the way of her trying to do her job.

Leandra walked back up onto the pitcher's mound and stomped on it. She was trying to get the red clay off the bottom of her shoe so she could keep her balance when throwing the ball. Leandra was really nervous, which was why she was checking on so many things. She was trying to calm her nerves. Then Leandra leaned forward and wound up and let the ball go. P.J. kept her eyes on the ball. She swung and hit it over into left field, where Jessica Thompson (#28) of the Cats was positioned. Jessica ran up and caught the ball before P.J. even had a chance to reach first base. With that, the Jacksonville Cats got the third out they desperately needed.

The Cats fans were making lots of noise in the stands, letting their home team know how happy they were for them. The score was still Tigers, four, and Cats, three. Now it was the Jacksonville Cats turn to hit and try to take the game. They knew this would be their last chance to become the champions and win the high school district championship.

Coach McCarthy told the Cats shortstop Alie Green (#4) that she was up first to hit, and Alie then took a deep breath and prepared herself before she going out to the batter's box. In the Tigers dugout, Coach Lawson and Coach Connie were telling the girls that this was it. "This is what we have been waiting for … We have to hold on to the one run lead."

Jany grabbed her glove and got ready to go back onto the pitcher's mound. But Coach Connie stopped her, and Coach Lawson said to Jany, "You have done an awesome job pitching, but we're going to let Adreena close out the game because she's good at doing that." Coach Lawson asked Adreena, "Are you ready?" Adreena told Coach Lawson, "I'm as ready as I'm going to be." Little did Adreena know she was about to pitch against the best hitters on the Jacksonville Cats team.

And first up was the Jacksonville Cats shortstop Alie Green (#4). She has always been rated one of the Jacksonville Cats's best home run hitters. Coach Lawson told Adreena, "All you have to do is strike the next three hitters out, and we win the championship." Adreena's teammates ran out onto the field ahead of her and took their positions. Then Adreena took a few deep breaths and grabbed her glove. She ran out of the dugout and took her position on the pitcher's mound. The Montiville Wild Tigers fans couldn't believe it—their own beloved Adreena Jones (#7) was getting ready to pitch—and they gave her a huge round of applause. That put a big smile on Adreena's face.

Adreena threw a few pitches to warm up with the Tigers catcher Candy Walker (#18). Adreena wanted to make sure that she and Candy were on the same page and knew what they had to do. The umpire yelled, "Batter up!" Alie Green of the Cats stepped into the batters box and took a few practice swings to warm up. She wanted to get the feel of the bat. Alie's favorite bat was the Louisville Slugger also—and boy, did she know how to use it. Adreena turned around to make sure all of her teammates were in their positions before she started pitching. Adreena threw her first pitch to Alie, and it was the famous change-up pitch. Alie swung and missed the ball. It hit Candy's glove hard and loud.

The umpire yelled, "Strike one!" Alie shook her head from side to side; she could not believe she had just missed that ball. Candy threw the ball back to Adreena, and Adreena had a big smile on her face. But she knew that it was just getting started and that she still had more work to do. Adreena settled herself down before she threw another pitch. Candy then gave her another signal to throw. And Adreena agreed with the pitch. So she threw the second pitch, and it was the uneven ripple ball that Adreena was well known for. Alie took a swing at it, and again she missed. "Strike two!" yelled the umpire. Alie was baffled as to why she was not hitting these pitches.

The Jacksonville Cats fans were also getting worried because Alie hadn't been able to hit anything Adreena had thrown to her yet. Adreena set up and threw her third pitch. Alie finally got a hit, and it was a line drive to the Tigers shortstop, Amy Banks (#55). Alie took off running for first base. Amy picked the ball up and turned and threw it to the Tigers first baseman, Jennifer Williams (#9). The ball reached first base just a little bit ahead of Alie. The umpire yelled, "She is out!" Adreena had one out on the Cats; she had stopped one of their big hitters. Now she had just two more outs to go, and the Tigers would win the game—and the championship.

The next batter up for the Cats was second baseman Christine Haggman (#33). Christine had won a contest for the most hits in the outfield and runs scored, so Adreena knew she had to be extra careful about what kinds of pitches she threw to Christine. Adreena was sweating like she had never sweat before. You could hear Paula yelling to Adreena from the dugout, "Girl, I got a joke for you when you finish!"

The umpire yelled, "Play ball!" Christine walked into the batter's box, and she placed her feet just right so she could get a good hit at the right time. Adreena threw her first pitch to Christine—the wild rock pitch. Christine took a swing at it and missed. "Strike one!"

Christine was beating the ground with the bat like crazy. You could tell she was really upset about missing the first pitch. Then Christine calmed down and stepped back into the batter's box. Adreena threw her second pitch, and it was coming to Christine like the flow of calm water, really smooth and quiet.

Christine squeezed the bat really tightly and stepped in to the pitch. She swung again. "Strike two!" And again Christine took the bat and beat the ground with it. The umpire yelled, "Time out!" He walked over to the Jacksonville Cats dugout and talked with the head coach. The umpire told Coach McCarthy, "You have got to calm your player down, or else she will be ejected from the game. If that happens, it's an automatic out."

Coach McCarthy said, "I'll take care of it." So Coach McCarthy walked out to the batter's box and told Christine, "You have got to control your temper or else the umpire is going to eject you from the game. That'll be an automatic out for us, and we can't afford that right now." Christine looked up at Coach McCarthy and said, "Okay, Coach. I understand." The umpire yelled, "Play ball!" Christine knew that if she didn't hit this next ball, she just might lose it. Adreena got another signal from their catcher, Candy, about what ball to throw for the next pitch.

Adreena waited until the Tigers fans had calmed down before she released the next pitch. The fans calmed down, and Adreena threw the next pitch. It was one that Christine had never seen before. It was called the drop-dead ball because just before it got to you it would just drop. Christine took a swing and missed again. The umpire yelled, "Strike three!" Christine raised the bat and started to throw it, but the umpire looked her right in the face. So Christine brought the bat down and shook her head and walked back to the dugout.

The Montville Wild Tigers fans were so happy they did not know what to do with themselves. Their home team was doing their job. And they had never seen a pitcher like Adreena who was just able to take control of the game. Mr. and Mrs. Jones were amazed at how well their daughter Adreena was playing this game and in such a professional manner.

Next up to hit for the Jacksonville Cats was designated hitter Denise Harris (#46). Denise was known for embarrassing pitchers in the last inning of games, and her well-known record had continued throughout part of the Cats season. Denise was one of the reasons the Cats have been able to get this far. Coach Lawson called a time out. He was aware of who was getting ready to hit next; he knew about Denise's record. Coach Lawson walked out to the pitcher's mound to talk with Adreena. He told her, "Denise doesn't play around—she is the best. So, if you want me to, I can pull you out and let Jany finish." Adreena told Coach Lawson, "No, I can finish with no problem." Coach Lawson then said to Adreena, "Okay, this is it. It's all yours, and no matter what happens, we played our best."

Coach Lawson walked back to the dugout and told Coach Connie that Adreena was okay; he had just needed to let her know what she was up against with this batter, Denise. The umpire yelled, "Batter up!" And out came Denise Harris in her crisp uniform. Adreena held the ball in her glove for a few seconds before she followed through with her pitch; she was very nervous. Adreena remembered what she had read about her favorite softball player, Viola Smith, and what she would do when she faced challenges. Adreena threw her first ball to Denise—the straight sharp curveball. Denise swung, and she hit the ball—but it was a tip. The umpire yelled, "Strike one!"

This made Adreena more nervous, and she wondered what was going on in Denise's mind. *Is she going to close this game out now? Or is she just toying with me?* The fans from both teams were standing up on their feet because this was the game of the century for them.

Adreena just stood there on the pitcher's mound in position and ready to throw her second pitch. And while thinking of what kind of pitch to throw next she thought about how much confidence Viola had showed when she played in her first professional baseball game. Adreena threw her second pitch, and Denise zoned in on the ball coming her way. She swung but missed the ball. The umpire yelled, "Strike two!"

Adreena got set to throw and had high hopes that when she threw the next ball it would be her last and final pitch of the season—and over for the Cats. She could bring home the championship title for the Tigers, or it could be that this game would go down as a tied championship game. Adreena was so stressed and in need of some kind of inspiration from somewhere that her imagination started to play tricks on her.

All of a sudden, as Adreena was getting ready to pitch, the wind started blowing, and something caught her attention. She looked up into the stands and thought she noticed a group of women sitting together. They all had "BHS" and numbers on their jackets, and the lettering on the back spelled "Burnsfield High School Class of 1936."

Adreena thought she saw all of the players from her favorite book: Susie Mulligan, pitcher; Wilma Jackson, catcher; Hattie Johnson, first basemen; Lucy White, second baseman; Mabel Green, shortstop; Louise Patterson, third baseman; Mattie Brown, right fielder; Mary Hunt, center fielder; Amy Gray, left fielder; Margie Moon, pitcher; Thelma Anderson, pitcher; and Coach Melvin Percy.

They were all smiling at Adreena. It got really quiet, and still Adreena's imagination was playing with her. She noticed someone else extra special, and that one special person walked down from the stands to talk with her. That person said to Adreena, "I know you know who I am." Adreena said, "Yes, I do," and with a dazed look on her face she continued, "You're Viola Smith, right?" And Viola said, "You're right."

And then Viola told Adreena, "You've been doing a great job in this last inning, and so has your whole team." Viola also told Adreena, "All you need to do is hold your head up high and throw the last ball and make it count. You have a special gift, and don't let anyone take that from you. You will go on to do great things in your life, Adreena. And you can be the best softball player you have ever been, if you just keep your head up and work hard at your gift of playing softball."

Adreena's imaginative sighting and conversation continued. Viola told Adreena, "Don't be afraid … Throw the ball. Just throw it." Viola asked Adreena, "Do you remember the last ball I threw in the big game I played in to help the Junction Clowns win?" Adreena said, "Yes, I do." Viola said, "Then you should take some cues from that game." By then, Adreena was standing on the pitcher's mound with a big smile on her face. And Viola said to Adreena, "One more thing … I think you are a great pitcher." Then Viola went back into the stands. She and all of her teammates and Coach Percy waved good-bye to Adreena and then vanished. And then everything was back to normal for Adreena, like nothing had happened.

As Adreena snapped out of the trance she was in, she could hear Coach Lawson saying, "Adreena, are you okay?" And she finally looked over at him and said, "Yes, Coach, I'm okay." Adreena threw the last pitch to Denise with all the confidence in the world; she had no doubts anymore. Denise swung at the ball and missed.

The umpire yelled, "Strike three—you're out!" Denise just stood there with a stunned look on her face; she could not believe that she had just struck out. Coach McCarthy and the rest of the Cats couldn't believe they had just lost the championship to the Tigers. The Montville Wild Tigers ran out onto the field from the dugout. They couldn't believe what had just happened. The Montville Wild Tigers had won the district championship. They are the new high school district softball champions.

The Jacksonville Cats had worked hard to get there. They had fought a good fight, but they just weren't able to pull it off to win the season championship. Both teams congratulated each other on a game well played.

Coach Lawson looked over at Coach Connie and said to her, "This is so amazing for us ... to finally make it here to district and then pull off winning the championship the way we did?" Coach Connie looked back at him with a big grin on her face and sais, "Yes, it is ... and it feels so good to have all of that hard work finally pay off."

Kim Peeler, the pitcher for the Cats, and Adreena, the pitcher for the Wild Tigers, were out on the pitcher's mound talking about how the game had been played. Both Mr. and Mrs. Jones were proud of how Adreena had ended the game. Coach Lawson and Coach Connie talked with the team when they returned to the locker room.

Both of the coaches wanted to say to the team, "What a way to end the season!" After Coach Lawson and Coach Connie finished expressing their feelings to the team about their big win, they decided to walk outside and let the girls enjoy their big accomplishment. Paula started walking around telling jokes as usual. Adreena sat on the bench in the locker room, still unable to believe what had just happened. The players' parents waited outside. And as each player left the locker room, they congratulated Adreena on a job well done. Soon the locker room started to get quieter and quieter.

Coach Lawson and Coach Connie walked back into the locker room, and Coach Lawson asks Adreena, "So what plans do you have for yourself after you graduate at the end of the school year?" Adreena said, "I don't know, Coach … maybe go to college and play softball." Coach Lawson and Coach Connie smiled at Adreena and told her that they liked that answer because she had a gift for playing softball and she shouldn't waste it. Then Adreena said to them, "I promise not to waste it."

Coach Lawson gave Adreena a hug and told her, "Good job tonight. Make sure you stay in touch after you graduate." Then Coach Lawson told Coach Connie that he was going to his office to pick up a few things and go home. Again Coach Lawson said to Coach Connie and Adreena, "Great game tonight." As Adreena was getting ready to leave, Coach Connie asked her, "Can you sit down for a minute?" Adreena said, "Sure, Coach. What's on your mind?"

Coach Connie said, "I've noticed for a while now that you have been reading that book in your backpack and you're really into it … I like the title."

Adreena then told Coach Connie that her mother had the book for her birthday when she turned nine or ten. "And I've loved it ever since then; it's a great book." Coach Connie then said, "It sure is," with a big smile on her face. When Coach Connie said that, "Adreena looked at her with a puzzled look on her face." Then Coach Connie said, "You see, Adreena, Viola Smith is my mother." And with wide eyes and a surprised look Adreena asked, "You mean, you are Viola's daughter?" "Yes," replied Coach Connie.

Then Coach Connie told Adreena, "You know that book you have been reading? Well, it's about my mother, Viola Smith. She is the best softball player that I have ever known." Adreena's mouth dropped, and her eyes got really big. Coach Connie then said to Adreena, "I would see you reading this book everyday, and I could see how much my mother would inspire you to work harder. And I knew you were going to be the best softball player you could be."

As Coach Connie and Adreena were talking, the science teacher, Susie Mulligan, the history teacher, Lucy White, and the librarian, Mable Green, came walking into the locker room. Adreena looked up in amazement. She didn't understand why they would come by just to see her, and then she looked over at Coach Connie and saw that she had a huge smile on her face. Then Adreena started putting it all together. Adreena remembered the posters that were in her science and history class and the sweater the librarian had worn that day.

In fact they all had on sweaters with the initials "BHS" on them, which stood for Burnsfield High School. Adreena then started saying, "Now it all makes sense to me. A few times, some of you tried to tell me about the sweater and poster and who all was in the poster, but we were always interrupted before you could finish."

Adreena couldn't believe that she was really meeting some of the Burnsfield Cats that she had been reading about. It was like a dream come true. Adreena started telling each of them how they had helped her become a better softball player and that they also helped her to rally her teammates to win the championship that night. Adreena was so nervous.

Coach Connie asked Adreena, "Are you okay?" Adreena nervously said. "Yes, except, I did not get to meet Viola Smith." Just as Adreena said that, someone came through the locker room door. It was Viola Smith, her all-time favorite softball player, the one she had been reading about for all those years. Adreena's eyes got really big, and she had a stunned and amazed look on her face. She began smiling from ear to ear. Adreena started shaking and was so excited that all she could say to Viola and her Burnsfield Cats teammates, with tears in her eyes was, "This season couldn't have ended any better than this." Adreena then got a big group hug from Susie, Mable, Lucy, and Viola.

All of a sudden, Paula came running back into the locker room because she had forgot her purse. She asked Coach Connie, "What's going on in here? And who are all these people?" Coach Connie explained to Paula what was happening and why they were there. Then out of the blue Paula said to Adreena, "So, those people in your book were real people after all, huh?" Everybody looked at Paula and started laughing.

Mr. and Mrs. Jones had begun wondering what was taking Adreena so long to come out of the locker room, so they went in to find out. Adreena introduced them to Viola and some of the other Burnsfield teammates. Mr. and Mrs. Jones's jaws dropped, and they said, "Is this really them?" Adreena's parent were surprised and happy to finally meet the people who had gotten their daughter so fired up about softball and helped bring out her gift for playing softball.

Viola and the other Burnsfield players told Adreena to continue to perfect her craft of softball and not let it go to waste but to put her talent to good use. Viola told Adreena that she liked how smart she was about playing her softball game and that she should continue to play that way. For Adreena that was a huge compliment, coming from Viola. Everyone continued to talk for a while and then said their goodbyes. Coach Connie told Adreena to stay in touch with her and Coach Lawson and to let them know how softball was going for her in college. Adreena said, "Okay, I will." And then she thanked Coach Connie for giving her the best surprise ever—the chance to meet Viola Smith, her favorite softball player.

The end of the school year finally came, and the Montville Wild Tigers had made history. This was the first time they had ever won a softball championship. After high school and graduation were over, the summer of 1983 could really begin.

One day that summer, Mr. Jones was watching TV, and Mrs. Jones was going over some papers from the bank. Adreena was upstairs listening to the radio with her headphones on. There was a knock at

A PITCHER TO REMEMBER

the door, and Mr. Jones answered it and asked, "May I help you?" "Yes, my name is Richard Tanner, and I'm the owner of the Florida Marlins baseball team, and I would like to invite your daughter to play with the Marlins."

Mrs. Jones heard what the gentleman had said from where she was sitting, and she quickly ran upstairs to get Adreena. Mrs. Jones was so excited she just opened the door of Adreena's room without knocking and ran right in. Adreena said, "Mom, are you okay?" Mrs. Jones said, "Yes, dear, but there is a Mr. Tanner downstairs and he wants to meet you!" So Adreena went with her mom downstairs and said hello to Mr. Tanner. And Mr. Tanner replied, "Hello, Adreena, Nice to meet you."

Then Mr. Tanner said, "Adreena, I watched you close out that big game against the Jacksonville Cats, and you did a great job. I have never seen such speed on a ball like that before—and especially not on a softball." Adreena told Mr. Tanner, "I don't know if I can throw a baseball that fast." Mr. Tanner said, "Adreena, don't worry about that. We have the best of coaches to help you out with that."

Mr. and Mrs. Jones were so excited about Adreena turning into a professional baseball player. Adreena would be the first black women in softball history to play professional baseball as a career. The Florida Marlins would be glad to have Adreena play for them. Later on that year, Adreena signed on with the Florida Marlins.

A couple of years passed by, and Adreena was fitting right in. Because she was such a versatile pitcher with a great pitching style, much of which she learned while playing for the Marlins, Adreena played for the Florida Marlins with all the confidence in the world. And in 1987 Adreena helped the team win the pennant.

Adreena would be known as the first woman to ever pitch in a Major League professional baseball game and the first to win a pennant doing so. Adreena S. Jones #7 … a pitcher to remember.

www.ingramcontent.com/pod-product-compliance
Lightning Source LLC
LaVergne TN
LVHW092055060526
838201LV00047B/1406